# THE CROSSING

# THE

# CROSSING

**ALAIN ALBERT**

GEORGE BRAZILLER
NEW YORK

I

*Daniel Peebles is dead. He was born in 1928 in a small country town in Mississippi. He left his family when he was seventeen, and he went to Europe. He lived some years in France and was sent to Korea as a soldier. He came back to the U.S. and he spent most of his time in New York, and then in California, before going back home down South. These pages are the journal he wrote while in the Psychiatric Hospital of J——, Mississippi. It could be a great help for those who would like to find out about the meaning of Daniel Peebles' life. Anyway he's dead now. He belongs to us. We can pull him to us, we can distort his life as we like. This is the matter.*

*About a month after he had come back South, Daniel Peebles was killed. It has to be said that Daniel Peebles was a Negro.*

3 o'clock. I'm tired. I have no courage. I just wanted to do something. Move. Show'em I wasn't asleep yet; but I wrecked it all. They've gotta protect themselves. They don't know I'm much less dangerous than what I do: They lock me in, they come and talk to me. I'm drunk. Stoned. I'm dead.

'Tain't my fault: when I arrived in my life it had already started; I didn't know what was going on. I began to live, as though I knew what had happened before; and I pushed the wrong buttons, I passed by the right people and I didn't know who they were.

Kids howling in the yards. Today bursts in my ears. The whole world's ready to burn. I wanna go! I'm

young! It's a mistake, I'm sure it's a mistake! . . . Don't
do that yet! . . . Leave me time! Leave me room!

I ain't been told what to do. I been put on the road,
not knowing whether I was supposed to swim, or to
walk. I plunged, and the ways are hard. Yeah folks, I
ain't that ugly! C'mon, look at me: say, am I any different?


I been beating that door, all morning round. It's
been childish. And useless. I won't ever walk again.
Ahma run away, all the time. And it'll end up like
that: burnt fields and pain in the legs, falling. . . .

This here is a psychiatric hospital. That's what they
call an asylum. I ain't been put here because I'm mad
though: I'm supposed to be hiding out. To protect me.
In fact, it protects everybody. Everything's allright. I'm
lucky in a way: 't could have turned out worse for me.
But this land is sweet. I heard I would probably have
been killed, if I wasn't here. I forgot all. I'm weak. I
bow my head. Soon I'll bow my shoulders. Native son's
back home. I shiver: 't could be fever, it's just fear. I
shoulda killed this guy: they wouldn't have got me.


Things ain't going fine. Ahma sleep. SLEEP.


Downstairs the kid's xylophone started to slide again.
All night that silly beat. I just wonder who ain't sleeping right now. And that damn sweet chorus, here!

**10**

Overthere space! Leave all! Fuck all! Be out there among the trunks, the air. . . . So many of my brothers are there, sleeping under them cabins. I'm tired of holding none but empty hands in my hands.

I can't walk. They keep me here, calm. I must not talk. Good tall niggers keep me silent. My brothers are afraid I'd sing again. Whites don't have to know how many black songs died, halfway to their spittle, and my long dark nurses are here to protect their light sleep. But I want to get out. I want to go. Boats in the hot morning's mist throwing their holler against my windows. And I'm barrel in the docks' shade, broken drum.

Steel burning slowly at noon. What ain't melting? A string of light, thin, crosses the bit of sky before the front building. A string, anything lightning the iron. Something's to be done. Drawn. Tomorrow again the same faces, the same smells, the same noises, the whole drag . . . If it don't explode Ahma get mad!

Write. Wait. Won't anybody answer these motherfuckers?

Lord! That other one downstairs gonna sing again. Two days they been tryna keep him silent. Two days they been strangling his bloody nigger's cry. . . . And his voice, his broken dream in the dust, his old black

11

dream murdered in the harbor . . . Close that door! Shut up. . . . And we're two here, to know that the sun is living. Between him and me, old mad, it's like a useless tin: the sun . . . and the water getting hard, rough to the skin. The flag . . . Shout brother, shout! Anyway we'll be castrated, soon or late. Don't lose no time.

Fifteen years ago I was here, and it was the same flat sky, the same dirt, the same torpor. I spent days lying in the shadow, watching the waterfront. Now they've put factories on the banks, just where we used to hide. . . . If it could rain again! Flood on all that, cleaning up everything, drowning them all. . . . Shit, a land neat like a kitchen . . . and trees. But it won't rain here. Forbidden.

There's a sonofabitch now in town that I'd like to find. Lord! He sure better go before . . .

How old am I? I seen so many faces. Pale yellow black. . . . Cops' faces and motherfuckers' faces. Dont-you wake me up I gotta right to sleep now, get back your sermons, all your stuff, little, so little ones! Dont-you wake me up! I had a brother in that fear, I had a brother in that light. And he carried in his chest more forests, more wind, more stream than never your brooks bastards will see. Let one of you tell me he was wrong!

Bow the head. Wait, I wanna sing, me too, like the other mad. . . . But I can't believe, I can't sing, I ain't got no word to carry from roof to roof. I make noise, I scream, but I can't say the tale. Just shit.

My name's Daniel.

If I could split . . . I wanna walk. I want ways in the shadow. A nurse comes in. She looks at me, slowly, like with compassion; she's looking for the hole in my head, the crack. . . . Doesn't understand. Now the sun again. Lord come a day, bring a blind's night real black with that density hitting the noons, and that strikes, strikes. . . . We dreamed of a country with roads solid like the train's rumor, with trees and rocks dancing, beating the stone, shouting. . . .

The guy, still on his piano. Three poor shy notes, always the same, all the time. He's got a point: something to do. His way. 'T would be time for me to have my way: staring at the roofs, the heavy steel in that summer, the light, neat alleys on the other side of town, and my brothers crawling, chewing the dirt, is that it? Who said I wanted to be a one-way man? Did I? And they've put me in the hospital. They'll cure me, I'm telling you. I'm real sick. Homesick.

No choice. That's a swinging place. Nobody never does anything but they all are SOCIAL creatures. Everybody watches himself slowly dying in the smiling mirror of his fear, and that's a way to recover. I'm writing, of course, but I'm crazy they said. Sweet people, sweet wonderland. I love you, cause you CAN hurt. You know the way: "Look at dese chillun on de bank. You want'em to live dontyou? You ain't gonna make no waves, you'd drown'em." . . . And you're packed. Simple.

Fuck all agonizing children! Ahma drown'em. I wanna see that even death won't make us get outta this dream.

Tears! Tears on them! They never touched a real ground, never drank real coffee. You didn't know babe, but even your sex was dreamy. You never fucked nothing but dreams, lousy nice-legged dreams.

News of the world. Birmingham Ala. June 12th.

NIGHTMARE COMES TRUE. Last night several Negroes woke up in the middle of the night and found out they could die and kill and make love and have cigarettes and sit down and be hurt and come blind right away and have no fun no soul no brothers and be packed and sold and strangle their children not to see them sold and know nothing about Jazz.

Birmingham White Citizens' Council made a report intending to establish the Communist responsibility in the disaster. If you can't brush your teeth after every meal use DENTAL.

Next information at 1:30 P.M.

Tuesday morning.

I woke up around six o'clock in the morning. The sun was on the river. I couldn't see it, but I know he was seeking me among the slums.

Howard came to see me yesterday. I dig this tall quiet cat. He doesn't talk too much: I can speak and forget that he doesn't listen to me. I guess all his life he'll look like a student. I don't think he's very intelligent, but he's no hipster. That's a point. The big trouble up North comes from the hipsters. All the others are real sweet nice people. Like:

"Frank I'm really thankful for the way you accepted me. I know I'm quite different, but still, America can be proud of you."

"That's allright boy. Don't make no problem out of it. But now tell me. There's a thing bothering me, which I wanted to know for a pretty good time. How can you recognize an African from an American Negro?"

Sweet. Sweet people. I'm telling you.

Now the whole forest burns under the midday. Shoes. More steps on the fields, and stands up, hitting the earth.

They put me downstairs last night. Now I've got a room of my own. Small but quiet. Only trouble: they

**15**

lock me in. I can't even go to the bathroom without calling; but I don't hate to be locked in. At least my so-called mates won't steal my things anymore.

The man in his cell. Room 19. Out there alleys among true trees. A dream. Looks like Europe a little. But Europe's so far. All places . . . Quiet Korean families sitting around low tables, and centuries of knowledge, cool sceneries with the frost on the top of them hills, and all that burning and we did put the fire on all that, and we killed, and we raped to defend Western civilization. And I thought I'd forget under the gray tenderness of Brittany. And I got high in New York. And I got busted and jailed in Seattle. Fifteen years the same circle of steps on unknown grounds looking for God knows what freedom while I just had to look around me where I had always been and see the snake of dust, the subterraneans under the harsh avenues.

I'm looking for cigarettes. For twelve days I didn't have any. It didn't bother me too much actually, but this morning I woke up with a terrible cigarette-will. I also want a typewriter, and I probably won't have none of 'em.

Hang your life to the words. Look at the rain inside the faces, beyond their skin. Who's gonna be able to close this door well enough to let people be dry again?

Fifteen years I been running away from here. Man I thought I could make it. I swear the Lord I thought I could destroy the power of this land on me. Probably it was possible, but I ain't seen enough night through my walk, I ain't seen enough fire, enough sun on shore. Always everywhere I found myself in front of the same frightening drawing and men slowly dying, strangled by their foolish hopes of kill the past, of be new, be others, kill themselves to leave room for the next hurricane.

That ain't life. Erection ain't love. And what difference can it make? What's the use of all that? Who's you, first, moaning in the fat belly of the earth? Why don't you run and lose time and give smiles and shake hands and say hello to the people you hate and take buses and struggle for a car, larger flat, more bread, more sex, less and less see the pure drawing, the too simple line under the mud, the mist, the chaos, your day-to-day blind's walk?

I'm wrong. People here don't even have time to be destroyed by themselves. Everything's been decided before they were born. One more black at the right of Charles Street, one more white at the left. And each life depending on the other one. And kids waken up in the midnight with an ocean of white faces over their fear, kids sent by their own parents to a hopeless fight against their pride. Kids walked over by a mob. Kids playing organ, straightening their hair, studying, studying and cutting and killing and beating drums, women, or just the ground. Kids whose anger is like dead flies upon a lake. Kids whose voices won't ever reach the cover of the box. And a whole people growing insane among more crazy nurses.

Saturday afternoon.

All these poor lives coming to hurt this morning like old dead ships against the fog. Guys who grew up with something different; they couldn't exactly say what it was, but they knew it was growing up with them. Something like not being able to sink into the common drag; and the something followed them at school, and then in their first hopeless jobs. And they lived, they had always lived with the idea that it would end up like that, here, that the something wouldn't find any place but this here.

Poor figures of turned-inside walk. The dark side of the moon: never seen. You can't get drunk outside, but here the doctors give you pills to get you high. I heard they now have real American hospitals, where you're taken care of, where you don't get high. It's a luck they haven't been extended to Negroes. Of course, here, it's pretty horrible. The process is: if you ain't mad yet, please be nice, become mad as soon as possible so we can calm you. But I don't know who is insane, the sick in the hospital or me making believe I am not. The families here are wonderful. They come twice a week, bring cigarettes and some sweets, and go back to their terribly concrete preoccupations. Don't you dare ask for anything else: they're always right. Anyway, they brought you here: how could they be but right? There is a cat two rooms farther who's been brought here by his parents because he didn't like church music. Another one because he didn't like his wife anymore, and SHE brought him here. Both of 'em HAD to be insane. Then the rule, the law is: forget all about normal life; be so that you'll be definitely depending on your sick pals, on the hospital, on your family's Thursday sweets.

Another thing is how they can make you feel that you got a plenty of time. Nobody's never in a hurry, nurses calmly planning about how it will be in two years, everybody trying to make you understand that since you're here, it'd be useless to do anything but wait, that a cure was to be done if you were living outside, but you're not, so you'll never be cured, and never be outside again. Everybody plays this awful game. Guys remembering their child's fears like you can only talk about'em through books. Fire's naughty ain't it, fire's naughty! Black chickens telling you how many whites they killed, how many whites came to excuse themselves after having found out how strong they were, how whites better take care when they talk to them. How educated they are. How many years they spent in New

York with a German girl. Telling you what famous singers they are. How many cars they got, and begging a roach. And everything to make it look natural, as though this is the real world, the real life. . . . Don't believe they're cured, since it's called Hospital. It's just a place where the mad are free to be as mad as they want. Every morning, every night, the pills make you COOL mads. In the middle of the day, you feel like being mad in your own way. Then, if that ugly mood doesn't fly away, an extra-pill arranges it.

Sunday morning.

I won't even go to the hospital church. The kind of stuff I'm afraid I couldn't stand. Like that other night in the Club. Looks like everything started right there and then. I still don't know what happened; I should try to find out; know why I tried to get outta the dream. 'T was too much probably, too close to the very picture, the image of what it had to be.

It's a drag. I write and everything starts to shine. Every word makes me farther from what the very minute has been. Silence. That's what it should be. Must be a way to write, without lying. Stay close enough to the blind rush, the furniture. . . . But you can't live that twice.

20

Nine o'clock. Morning stretching out behind the branches. Sunday morning: people glad, once a week, to wake up early. Enjoy the day, show they ain't got nothing to do. Sunday morning: the hospital full of holy sick.

Could I pray again? I loved to pray when I was a kid. I didn't really care for all them stories of bearded Jews and birds and lambs, but I enjoyed church, the stiff touch of my uncle preaching, the fat women swinging their heavy breasts along with the music, and the long sorry faces they had in the streets, the same ones, as though they never had no breasts. . . . What's the use now? God ain't black, and he can't be white. . . . I don't give a damn. . . . All that crap about you must love your brother . . . I got to love him: I can't hate, they stole the meaning of my hatred, saying that a nigger was naturally hating, naturally mean. But I can't love either: I don't feel like it.

This hospital sure is a nice place. Nurses act toward sick like whites toward Negroes. They've found blacker than them. Being with the mad makes'em feel superior. They know they ain't too bright, but at least they are sane. A couple of years ago I met a French West Indian. He told me that some cracker in Georgia told him he was West Indian, and different, but that American Negroes were just wild beasts. So was I considered by the nurses: mad, but a different kind. They come and

21

explain to me that they've been working here for ten years. They KNOW the mad. They still have toward me a little prejudice. I am different, but I'm mad as well. My friend was different, but still his skin was black.

Monday afternoon.

New week . . . And what does it mean? Every day has been sounding on the ground like notes, deep in the running land. What does anything mean? We been dreaming of the time of no-time. The tall figure alone on the green side of the cliffs and talking to the sun, pure, gone out of time and hours and days and seasons and goings and comings. No time. I know it could happen: uniform gray light on the lines, the yards, and moveless glance, shades becoming hard labor of the earth.

It's been raining all night long. At last. Ways among pines, turning under the carriages, dust tracks under the wheels. Somewhere it's been night and gloom. Drunkards swinging between the walls, and the whole dark blowing, plunging into the blue.

Wednesday afternoon.

It was a long narrow room. Dirt on the walls, smoke and spittle in the air. I'd been there hours, years, centuries. I'd been there all night, and the whole night had been there, in my life, forever, but I just didn't know it. There were tables, beer, stoned waiters, stoned customers, stoned musicians and song about all. People sleeping on them chairs, exhausted. Buddies laughing, drinking, dancing, brothers getting higher, deeper, farther. And it was not time. I can tell you, I know: 't was not time but the beat, it was no time but the chords and it stopped while they broke. It was the whole dream made dreamier, appearing. Faces sending back the electric light, dancers suddenly falling on the floor, and stream among all that, stream in this stoned world, trying to make it move, stream tired, dying softly at our feet.

And I'd nevermore be outside again. I wouldn't be in the sun again. I knew I was gonna live more nights like that one; I was BACK, after fifteen years turning 'round. I been scared. None didn't move: everybody was already beyond the bursting, following their changes. And I knew it had started. I knew this howl was coming from deep in the buried years. It was going up along my back, it would soon reach my throat and it would have to burst then, bleed on the floor, the tables. . . . They began to blow and it floated above the room, wide; it was printing the blue on the walls, coming back, splitting again and coming back, stubborn sentence in the nerves, crushing all, weighing on our heads. And it was coming inside the voice, it was swinging into the words, it was laughter, bitter bursting. And I saw everything suddenly, the whole place with its small small life and myself, slowly moving inside the dream, hitting

23

unreal shapes, and no man, no hand around. . . . And that was too much. From that very moment it had been too much. Lonesome sidewalks under the light, rain shining on the soil and that cat's voice digging a tunnel in the bare crops . . .

*"Early one mawnin . . ."* Say it babe! One's gotta talk for all that. Someone's gotta say how these lives, why the cold, why the winter without coats, why cats whose souls were taken off by years of wait, of be cool of bow the head of bow the back of suck the dust of keep your place. . . . *"De Blues come fallin down. . . ."* Thick trunks outside. Beings like masses of rock, solid, sitting on their past, the ass on their light crossings. And we been dragging the rest, begging, feet hardly drawn off the mud. *"Early one mawnin . . ."* We ain't gonna have no more mornings. We been laughter, joy, we been fire. Stream's gonna leave us, and we be dry, dry. . . . *"Cause I'm prison bound. . . ."* Listen babe, it won't last all the time, this is gonna sink in between our lives and we can't hold it. Chords now, notes tearing the glass. Tell'em man. If you break you dead! Keep on pouring your song in the shade. Lines of yelling kids out there. Say why anger so strong, so true, say why hatred sometimes and striking in the gate, and abortive violence too. . . .

I been scared. He was singing and it was too much, too naked, too far. You can't push a life out its own borders, cause it can get stuck, and turn over the day,

24

and fight and die. My whole life had been tending to that minute. All my days, millions of seconds pulling them roads, and the song had never changed. I'd been away but it had stood still, I'd been out but it was just a break. And I felt the holler ready to fly, leave my throat. I saw. Smallening figures in the bar, and the shout made stronger, higher, and it tumbles down, grazes. . . . Don't you scream, it's a paltry violence. . . . Shit ain't there some'n to do? But why don't you move, bunch of docile motherfuckers? Why don't you shake the powder off your nights . . .

There were people in that room. A whole lotta people. . . . And their movements were like powerless waves dying on the banks.

I felt something like a cold wind around me and cats suddenly getting cooler, laughter blowing out, bodies tired right away, empty glances and the heads deepening, sinking into the shoulders. . . . Two whites were standing by the door. I saw them, and everybody was seeing them at the same time. The guy next to me whispered: "Whut de hell is dey doin here?" I looked at him. He was tall, too young. . . . "I don't know!" A guy meets another one and there ain't no light of this life he wants to dig. Two words make a bridge but one of'em sides will always be shade. He knew I was looking at him, he was standing my look and waiting. I'd have like to tell him. . . . I ain't got no time. . . . I

don't wanna make anybody lose time. . . . I'm somewhere else! I'd have liked to make this guy look at my
way; put him alone in the dryness of that road and let
him walk on it a little. . . . Scream a little. . . . But it
was the wrong moment, the wrong place, and I wasn't
even sure it wouldn't be wrong cat! . . . And there we
were, awkward, like prisoned in our fear of fire. I
wanna talk to him. I love him. I try to smile and it
sounds false. We must have something to share, it's not
possible that I'd be so far. . . . "Near Jackson, you know,
a little town . . ." He don't know. The flash in his eyes
vanishes. We go back to our sleep. One more missing.
I'm angry like a kid who's lost his toy. . . .

What the hell are those whites doing here . . . They
probably foreigners. Still, to look for chicks, this ain't
the right place! . . . I don't know. . . . Everything shines
before it disappears, I don't know whether they should
live or not, be so or not, I don't know what's worse, a
southern protestant or a northern hipster, I don't know
whether they should keep their place or not, whether we
should marry their sisters or just fuck'em. . . . The guy
is drinking now. He's white. Big deal. He's white.
Whatever he does he'll always be white; it sticks to him,
to his gestures, to the way he eats or makes love. . . . He
looks like a countryman. He knows what a tree is. He
probably keeps hidden in his depths the memory of
quiet torrid footpaths, the yard of a farm drying in the

afternoon. . . . He's like me! But he's WHITE. So what?
. . . He ain't but another man of the fields. That's what
he is. He probably keeps hidden the same games, the
same songs. . . . And he comes back home late in the
midnight feeling white, superior. I hate him.

He knows. He's been watching me all the time. He's
looking for me. Seek, white man, seek! . . . I know you
dig playing the dog. I can make you go wherever I want
you to go. I can make you feel good, or sad, I can make
you laugh and I can make you get mad. I'm the
master. You gotta know that. You'd better get used to it.
You don't decide no more. You made me the master!

Pink sleepy face. Primitive sonofabitch. He thinks
this is His place, he gotta right to call it Home. He just
don't know he could have been born Japanese, and get
lynched on the coast. Too bad in a war you don't have
time to look at the enemy's reasons: there is a whole lot
I would have liked to know about this cat, has he been
homosexual, does he like cornflakes, has he got any
brothers and sisters, has he ever been up North, does
he make love very often. . . . I knew I was following the
wrong track. I should have stopped then, let the night
talk for me, let this sonofabitch go back to his farm, his
square dances; but I needed him as much as he needed
me, and for similar reasons. I needed his hatred and
contempt to exist and he couldn't live without me be-

**27**

cause I was supposed to give him a role, a part to play, because I was an excuse for him to be something else than just himself.

He looks at me again. Weird world. We speak and we don't know how to speak. The life stays much beyond our poor sentences and we're so used to it now that we know, right away we replace one word by another, we know we gotta cross them words before we get to the flesh of our acts.

I'm too stupid. I can't even see a man without trying to make him come into my life or to go into his. Man! What kind of relationship do you have with your glass when you get drunk? This is no ethics, this is thirst.

Look at the things, at the men, one by one, never trust'em; that's what this guy is afraid he'll have to do with me, and that's what he doesn't want me to do with him. He gotta belong to something, any shit where he'd be no particular man. . . . He's been smelling me. And we both know there ain't enough room for both of us in such a fucked up world. We happen to be just the kind of individual that we've always been hating, since the early hatreds of childhood.

And this fucking time that doesn't walk. Still hours and hours to live before dawn, and each minute is a hard work of the shadow in us, every minute's gotta be won against the fear. We go in our lives like fishes in a tank, trying to cool it, to hide the stiffy rush, but fear has been let the night before, meaningless pack put on a table, and we make believe we don't care, but the mere step is already poisoned.

At this moment I knew it would go very fast. Funny how we prepare ourselves for our acts, we talk about'em, we try to make them important, big and grave, we swell'em and they happen so fast we're already on the other side, a little dazed, running after them, having missed them. I got up and went straight to him. He looked at me with his little white air, and I knew that beyond what he would say he meant "What's the matter Sam? Need any white help?" but he didn't talk. I tried to be as submissive as I could, as nigger as I could.

"Good evenin suh!" I said.

His buddy wasn't as drunk and came from somewhere else. He must have seen the danger in my voice right away. He pulled his friend by the arm, silently but his eyes were saying "let's go, come on! Got enough of nigger mood for tonight. . . ." My man turned toward him and said in an absent tone:

"You can go back now if you feel like going, Jessie . . . I join you later."

Everybody was watching us, waylaying us. I knew they all were much more afraid of what I would do than of him: we were reaching the extreme frontiers of the dream; they knew how dangerous it was. They didn't want the real life: someone had told them they were not quite ready for it. The one called Jessie went. Take care of yourself white man, you don't know nothing, you think one can avoid just by leaving. . . . You just a babe!

Now we were at our business. He was in front of me, though he would have like a situation which would have shown his superiority. But we were on the same floor, we were dressed the same, perhaps there was in his bearing a little more tightness, a little more cecity, but a Martian wouldn't have noticed any difference between us. . . . Oh! Yes. There was a difference. Our skins. Our skins didn't have the same color. My skin was brown and his was pink. That was a difference anyway. Yessuh, dere sho wuz a dif'rence.


He wasn't a natural southerner. He was a traditional extraordinary southerner. . . . The kind of cracker that writes books about spades and Jazz, that's so sorry not to have ever had a single colored friend, the kind that's so sincere. . . .

"Will you have a drink?" asked he.

"Yessuh sure!"

He wasn't too smart: he ordered a scotch without knowing whether I wanted one or not. He tried to have a courteous expression and said:

"Are you from here?"

I was disappointed he'd start the conversation right

away. I'd have like to drink calmly my free scotch first. . . . Too bad! I replied:

"Yessuh. I'm from here."

"Have you ever been up North?"

"Unhhunh."

"I reckon you must like it better up there. . . ."

"Why? Are there any reasons why I wouldn't like it here? Maybe you gonna tell me what I must like and what I must not like. . . ."

"That's not what I mean, not at all, I just want . . ."

"You're askin questions. Is it for the cops, the Klan, or you just plannin to write a book about the average Negro's mentality?"

"Listen MR. . . ."

"Peebles."

"Listen Mr. Peebles, I'm a friend of your race. . . ."

"WHAT RACE?"

"Well . . . I mean . . ."

"Wutcha meanin man?"

"I mean . . . the colored People. . . ."

I looked at his face, leaving my glance upon his eyes. He was feeling insecure, he was advancing in an unknown land and the soil was moving under his steps. He was afraid to speak, and he was afraid not to speak. He was ridiculous. But above all, he wanted to stay white. He wanted our relationship to be faked by this knowledge; perhaps he thought I would consider like an honor his coming down from all his whiteness to

**31**

talk to me! . . . In a way, he was lucky I had been the one he met. Even down South, young men's anger is a bill hard to pay. . . . I tried to be cool and asked:

"Do you wanna have a drink?"

He flipped. 'T was probably the first time he heard this question from a Negro. . . .

"No . . . no. . . . Thank you verymuch!"

He had signed his death sentence. I had given him one chance to be a man, just a man. But he wanted to be a WHITE man. Awright. Ahma be a niggah. Prob'ly de meanes' niggah you eve' met. And he knew. He knew we were gonna play the roles our fathers and grandfathers had always been playing for the greatest satisfaction of the nation. He was gonna play the one who believes he's white and I was gonna play the one who's been told he's a Negro.

"Mebbe you don't want no nigger drinks?"

"Don't get excited boy! No fire around. . . ."

"Wutcha want?"

"Listen, I can go wherever I like. . . ."

It was coming. I knew it was coming. I had pushed him and he was obeying me. We both were worth something else, but we were trying to reduce ourselves to familiar figures, trying to look like what we would be if we were nobody in particular.

"You better go wherever you like as long as you can. Pretty soon, I'll be the one who can go wherever he likes and throw the sonofabitches outta the club. . . ."

32

"You're damn lucky you're talkin like that to ME!"

"Yeah! I know. . . . You ain't no'n but a poor white trash!"

"Listen, nigger, this ain't New York, and you's talkin to a white man. Take care. . . ."

There we were. At last. It had been long, cause the cat was a little drunk, and in a pleasant mood, but he had been a toy. . . . I was starting to enjoy the scene really, when I dug the empty room, musicians gone. . . . Perhaps one of'em chickens already called the cops. . . . I knew it was dangerous, but I was drunk. . . . I wanted to break something in the flat wall of these lives. . . . To move, hit that pink fat face in front of me. Talk. Once. Just one time. Talk for the silence of so many years.

"Why would I take care? A coon don't talk like that to a white cracker sonofabitch? Then I prob'ly ain't a coon!"

"Don't bug me nigger, I could make you regret . . ."

". . . hangin me in your woods . . . But who told you you'd get outta here alive?"

The man started to feel nervous. After all, I was drunk enough to do it. Anyway, I was a strange nigger; he didn't understand me very well.

"You wouldn't touch a white man. . . ."

"Who talkin 'bout that? I'm talkin 'bout touchin you!"

I could feel his fear between my fingers. I was holding him, pressing there a little more, releasing the pres-

**33**

sure here. . . . He was sweating. . . . I thought: Mr. Cracker nigger-lover is scared. He never seen a spook so close. He scared to death. He looked at me with trembling lips, and I knew he could have done anything, he could have shot me right there or started to cry, he could have gone out running and shouting, or just sit down without a word. I knew that man was sick. I was about to laugh and cut out. He tried to get over his dread and started to yell:

"Nigger, if you touch me they's gonna lynch your motherfuckin black ass. . . ."

"They'd better do so! But you ain't gonna see it."

I was having a ball. All of it sounded like a joke. He was more and more scared. I knew if he hadn't been a white man in front of a darky, he woulda run away like a kid. But he hadda keep on being white. . . .

"You's one of the most stupid niggers I ever met. Let me go!"

"You really don't wanna have a drink? I'm payin!"

And something had already blown out. I could play as much as I wanted with that motherfucker. I was black. He was white. Wouldn't nobody touch him if he killed me, and wouldn't no black man down here keep alive after having touched him. I felt myself slowly becoming blind, I was burning right away. That stupid ass had dragged me down in his goddamn dream of death and I hated him. . . . His voice kept on urging me to do something. . . . Anything.

"Is you gonna lemme go nigger bastard?"

He was surprised by the first stroke. He didn't expect me to hit him so soon. Then I thumped again, and my whole life was jumping on his face. Dread. Thirty years of dread were getting their meaning through my hands. I hit, and it was for having had to wait thirteen years before I could go to school, I hit and it was for all my brothers and sisters who would hate me because of what I was doing, I hit and it was for the self-hatred that had been put into our souls by a smart white hand, it was for all my brothers cutting because they had no guns, all the gangsters in this town killing their brothers because violence had been put into their lives with such a strength, it was for the way I had been hating my family as a kid, just because they were as black as I was, and they were making believe one could live with it, and die with it, and never howl the meaning of our empty acts, never look in front of this truth that our acts were happening in the sweet land of the dream because it was the only one they had let us. . . . I hit because it was good, because I had never enjoyed anything more than hitting that poor fucked up white kid who had thought it was easy to be a nigger-lover!

I don't know what happened then. . . . I was looking at my act and I couldn't recognize it. I had wanted it to be a hole through which I could breathe, and it was already past, dead. I had been fooled. The guy wasn't even dead, but the whole town was looking for me. My good friends took me here. I let them do. I enjoyed the car ride. I like cars.

There ain't nothing in this here world to be done. I dig them pills. They make you sleep. SLEEP!

I feel good. Maybe because I've been remembering the whole thing. . . . Like it's supposed to be clearer now. . . . Like nothing there should bother me anymore.

And there we go . . . floating . . . lost in unununderstandable streams . . . words not sticking to the beat . . . our life yessuh it's like them days done gone . . . the fear we had to look at the instant . . . and it goes . . . floating . . . carrying gravel . . . grazing the banks . . . tumbling down . . . and I wanna scream . . . say it again it was too short . . . it was great man it swang . . . like there ain't nothin now to be done but get higher and die . . . and it goes . . . carrying rocks . . . floating . . . young young young oh young . . . and tired tired and oh tired . . . and I believe this damn scene is too much . . . and it crushes down there . . . nasty right away with bad glances . . . and it goes again . . . same trunks on the river . . . going down to the sea . . . floating . . .

Ahma get outta here. I don't care what happens. My life is there, floating above me, and I gotta go and catch it, and make it mine.

Wednesday night.

In a couple of hours Daniel Peebles will have escaped from the Negro Psychiatric Hospital of J——, Mississippi.

# II

Looks like the sun is sinking into the branches now, almost dead yet, dancing, cut in bits of tumbling light, with the tall trunks desperately shaking their long black fingers. The swamps . . . It was five o'clock when he got out of the sleeping hospital, it could be about five-thirty now, he didn't know, every minute was falling on his back like a disaster, he had gotten rid of time. He didn't know whether he was walking, running, or just dreaming this other fugitive sleep. It was coming into his memory, all, the trees along his walk, the dry stones of the way, the cabins vaguely profiled behind the fields, it was slowly accumulating the fluid mud in him. And he was listening to the furious sound coming out of his steps, it was singing and bouncing under his feet.

*"Tell me . . . Tell me baby how long it's been . . .
Since you BEEn home. . . ."*

There he was going again. To the same grimace
bursting among the furrows. Full ditch and the moon
streaming down in bloodstained tears, with the marsh
that suddenly stands up . . . Black . . . Black . . . His
whole body tightens in the wind, it's like he can't make
any more difference between this talking land and his
skin. His shoes dig the footpath and leave in the night-
soil small shining crescents, the dead eyes of his run.
And he knows this too. He hears the words pushing
their beat in the weed. . . . Now's the time! Now's the
time!

He sees the railroad track, naked, a little terrifying,
too fast glance crossing the country. He keeps on walking along, below. He knows every inch of ground can
hide him, because the whole soil belongs to his days.
He's coming back to the dark crops of his childhood, to
the slow ruin hitting against the palings, the low roofs
hardly going up beyond the canes, the evenings breathing the manure.

Day rises. The day beats his ears. Up there he can
see lines of trees slowly cut out of the bare sky, lights
blowing out, the little morning's breeze caressing the old
walls. On the hill behind him, just above all that, the
hospital stands still, surrounded by trees and lights, and

42

it's like snow covers the fields: the mist melting with the ground, people waking up and breathing down the dawn. *The light's behind them hills* he thinks, *and knows he's moving.*

He feels something inside the earth, swelling, like a long pain going down along the mountain's back. *I wish them cats leave me alone a li'l while.* He walks. *In the daylight it ain't goin to be as dangerous. . . .* He left the footpath and started to walk along the field. *"I know I heard a church bell tone. . . ."* *Them tunes just won't get outta my mind!* There was a kind of triumph, of deep agreement in that walk. *I'm runnin away! I'm runnin away!* He already knew everything would mix up in his steps. *Ahma cut that way outta the silence. Make it sound. . . .*

It must be about three hours he's been walking. The scene doesn't change verymuch. The same old narrow roads, all the time, and no soul around. . . . He doesn't feel tired. He is kind of resting while his legs bear the whole sunny drag. It was quite easy to get out of the hospital; they must not worry about people running away. Just the wall was a little bit difficult. But they all were sleeping so good. . . .

He got to cool it right now. Wait for he's made up his mind about what he's gonna do. He ain't got much money. He can't leave the state. *Fuck them excuses, I don't wanna leave anyway!*

**43**

He saw the two men in their car a little too late. He couldn't afford to run away or to hide. He kept on walking, just a little slower, and he was thinking terribly fast while trying to look like a useless detail in the scenery. *Where do I come from What will I say if they ask me I gotta be sure right now I got to cool it I gotta look stupid I could go to them by myself and tell'em any jive no it wouldn't work Perhaps they ain't even gonna pay no attention to me Oh yeah they will Crackers kind of feel cats like me They know somethin's wrong between us If they know about me I'll have some hard time!*

He was walking and his whole life was happening somewhere else. *I must not show'em I'm afraid I must not even look at'em.* He tried to figure out who they were . . . perhaps looking for him . . . no they look like something else. . . . *Shit I don't give a damn!* The fields were showing their long burnt body to the new morning. He remembered the run he used to do from the farm to the store, cutting behind through the woods. . . . Them times was no fun babe. . . . He looks up the brown furrows, seeking something to think about, trying to escape the fear. But he knows he can't, he knows some part of inside his glance is shivering in the dried mud.

He used to stay hours there, in the yard, sitting on the stairs among the chickens, watching the hills. That was a moveless world, with nothing but the sound of

44

wooden flutes or stovepipes or whatever it was and everything was solid and thick like a one-wayed village very far and poor. . . . Cats alone in their meaningless dance, no bridge between their hands, their shut smile close to the blood the rush in the blood and poured onto the soil . . . Hours slowly drawing steps in the dust.

*I gotta do some'n* . . . it can't work like that! It was a very old car, coughing and bouncing on the road. They looked at him and he felt the string of their sight digging his back while he was going ahead, swinging his shoulders from left to right. There was a kind of soft sigh then, and he was afraid to look at the smallening car behind him, afraid to stand up again. . . .

Once they had sent him to get he doesn't remember what at the drugstore at night. . . . He didn't wanna say he was scared to go out in the darkness. . . . Three days after that night they had lynched Maurice Walker who was accused of the murder of that white man from Clarksdale. . . . He was out in the streets when he saw the people starting to get nervous and to run in all directions. That day the fear had come into his life while he was running home on the narrow way with the fury of the mob sounding in his veins. And he had known right away that he was dying on that way, that his body was being burnt at the same time as Maurice's, that he was lying overthere, in the streets, among the screaming women. . . . He was eight: he knew dread wouldn't ever leave him, his life would now happen in this dead dream of violence.

He started to feel hungry. . . . Watermelons and bananas were passing through his head. He was tired too, but he had nothing to do with his walk; it was happening by itself, the same loud beat on the ground, and his song riding the bars.

It was in summer, everything had been dry for months, folks were almost getting mad. It was a terrible year. Hadn't nobody heard about no rain for more than a hundred days. . . . When they found that man in the river, they didn't think he'd been murdered, but Maurice was a damn chatterbox, going around telling folks that he was pretty glad that old rascal was dead and wouldn't bug nobody no more, that he wouldda done it if the Lawd hadn't taken care of that ol' sonofabitch! . . . When it appeared that he'd been doing some business with the white man found dead among the pebbles, the heat helping, it got crystal clear for everybody that Maurice had killed the man. They came and picked him up late in the afternoon. He didn't even try to resist, or to run away. This got them real crazy. They wanted to enjoy a little, that damn summer had been so flat, and that motherfuckin nigger bastard was trying to steal their lynch. Some of'em even wanted to let him go. It was no fun! So they took him way across town, claiming they just wanted to protect him, but in fact leaving the time for the others to come. . . . It was smart enough, because Maurice thought he had a chance to make it. While they were talking he hit the one who held him and started to run away. . . . It was all they expected. . . .

Nobody at home had talked about it. Nobody had talked about it at school. Nobody in the streets and the stores. . . . It was enough to see the threatening edge of the dream tearing their faces, the hole in their glance sometimes, the terrifying hole in their sleep.

*I wish I'd know where I'm goin!* . . . every inch of ground has found back its deep measure of steps and there he is, lost at last in a timeless land. *Now they've found out I'm gone, I gotta take care. . . .*

Why that? He thought that what he had lived would keep him away from it! Had he wanted to come back? What was the very hidden drawing in all that? *It belongs to me. Whatever it is it's mine.*

He had met Gloria one day on the way to the store. She was living in town actually. It was later, he didn't think of Maurice anymore; just sometimes he'd remember the long silent walks they used to have, the man and the boy, and sometimes the boy would take the man's hand in his. Maurice had burnt. Something small

**47**

and windy had burnt in the boy too. Gloria was fifteen, she wanted to be a teacher. Also she didn't want to go to church. When he first saw her he was thirteen. He was in love with Gloria; he used to say he would marry her so he could learn all the things she knew. Gloria was Maurice's sister; when she started to spend all her nights in town, right after her brother's death, her mother said she didn't want no girl like that at home. She went up to Chicago. She's in jail now. . . . She was a tall high-brown girl. She was a sweet chick. Just she didn't like church.

*I have to watch. I could lose myself in that walk. I have to keep my end in mind. It's too easy to walk like that, just walk and never mind the shadows in the ditch.* He has nothing. No bag. He's going. It's hot now. 'T might be about midday . . . or later. . . . He doesn't know. He doesn't care. Something in him just got free, like breathing better, with no look at the crashed watch behind him. And he knows that's his road, he never left it, he's never been away, he knows each branch, each stone, the whole sand running down on the meadow, filtering through the infirm branches.

He wakes up. He knows he's been sleeping. He just can't remember when it started. He was walking on a road and the road became unreal, he was hungry. . . . How had he come to sleep here? . . . The hay cracks in his ears. . . . It's night. *I'd better go.* . . . He feels something in his hand. . . . A bit of fruit half-eaten . . . He just can't see nothing in all that dark. . . . He ain't got no matches, no lighter, nothing. . . . And suddenly he's walking again, but in the dark. The night bathes his face, all is tall right away, tall. . . . He wants to talk but the words dry and fall. . . . *Man it's too much.* . . . He's falling too he can't help falling and it lasts and he falls and that ground is so far and GODDAMNIT and he walks again but he's been down and he keeps on walking and falling and he's bloody all over and he walks and he WHAT'S THAT JIVE walks and walks walks walks. . . .

He's sitting on the slope. A little bit of flesh is hanging from his cheek, he can feel the warmth of the blood on his hands. He sucks his fingers and breathes something of his jubilation in the sharp night. The blood starts to dry on his lips and it splits all around his mouth. *It's coming* he says, but he doesn't know. He's going back to the walk. The night is inside his flesh, there is no skin between . . . he's free . . . no day . . . no time . . . he walks, knowing he can fall and talk and laugh and walk again, leave the road, go and be back, he knows his sound wasn't written in no sky, but he's printing it in that night.

Slowly his fingers caress the face, the edges of blood dried along his chin. Something is breaking in the string of that moment. He's there, he goes ahead and

**49**

it's like his knees crush the earth, with the blood drawing on his skin small dry bites, and a fall happens, that he doesn't know. Sometimes it gets too bare and he feels the song trying to burst, pushing its waves against the silent body of his run. *Your time was to go. . . . Yell at the hills. . . . Your mission was to know!* Something in the line up there, like a nappy flow among the vague crests of his glance, just gets rid of all the meanders, all the turns, and becomes straight whip of the hills.

Maurice . . .

The road is a little wider now, starting to go down. Another valley . . . Other cities, and the same farms, the same stores, the same sidewalks.

It had probably been a weird moment, with the faces around him, so close in their disorder, twisted in the rage, and the furious features getting right away too near, letting appear all the softenings, all the cowardice, the pure hatred, the lowness sweating from each contraction. There had probably been a minute, perhaps just a second where he realized, he could see himself be out of the naked ugliness. There'd probably been a part of his life they couldn't go in, they couldn't rape.

He stiffens in anger. *Motherfuckers! Sons of bitches!*

*If you wanna git me the same you better be smart . . .
trashes!*

He walks. Looks like the night won't advance. And beyond his steps he knows he is taking with that ground a physical contact that's going to stay still. Muddy, turning over the dead blood of his days. It's the very last moment of the glance. He doesn't know where the flood starts and the earth stops, he doesn't know the borders of his night, but he gotta bundle that walk up, bow his sleep in the stream, fall again, go.

*I got a damn headache* he says, and it sounds like he's getting to something quite important, something like the very body of his run. . . .
He knows that taste. Everything always happens like he needs it. As though he couldn't live without that intensity in the throat, the sound on the countryside like the nerves on a leaf, and his walking in the night, his will to keep on walking, on going ahead.

He had heard Gloria calling him but he didn't want to go. Like he knew something was going to die. But she had said again "come" and he had taken her hand, he was walking at her side and he had the feeling he should be proud to walk at her side but he was not; he was just a little bit afraid to go back home too late. . . .
She was a little taller than him. She's good lookin he

**51**

thought. She sho is. He was calm enough. Ahma tell'em I hadda wait fer Ol' Will in the sto'. They ain't goin'a say no'n. . . . He thought of Maurice suddenly. She don't look like her brer verymuch he thought, and he tried to look at her like men look at women, but he knew her too well, she was just like another boy.

Another day is going to rise. He's sleeping sometimes, without knowing it, while still walking, and he wakes up and he's walked one more mile and he knows he's meeting a life on the road for which he'd been waiting; he's getting closer to the stone, the breath of the stone.

Perhaps ain't nothin goin'a happen he had thought. Maybe we's just gonna walk like we did before. . . . He'd have liked to speak, ask her, but he didn't want to break her move. Suddenly, while they were walking on the dark narrow way with nothing but branches and the night around them, she had asked: You want . . . right here? He had felt a kind of ice bullet in the stomach and thought again that he should be proud. But he said Yeah . . . right here, and he thought like that I'll be back home on time. She took off her dress and he was standing in front of her, thinking that somebody could come and see them, while something whispered in his head. Ahma fuck her. She wants me to fuck her!

It's daylight now. The blood beats his head, he's heavy heavy he knows he can't walk anymore he gotta be one with the ground. He leaves the road, he's crossing a field, and he falls among the corn and his whole face is bleeding and the sky is above him he's lying under the dry dawn. Asleep. And the deeper he gets the more it cries. He doesn't know whether he sleeps or not. His life has become a loud beat and he can't but shout along with it. Vaguely, he knows he is dreaming now, but it's all mixed up, he doesn't try to know, to understand, to see . . . he just keeps lying there, listening. . . .

Take care of yourself she had said. And she left. He's alone in the little frozen morning, she's going, he's alone in the lonesome farmyard with the ache in his shoulders. Ain't goin nowhere babe, all places is the same. It's something like the laughter in the noise and that long note tearing the path. She goes. He's alone with his naked dreams spat upon the dust of that old familiar road. People go around, carrying their little bag of trouble under their hair, well prisoned. That's the white man's world my son! Bullshit. Bullshit. The ache in his chest. You gotta go to the john sonny that's all! That's all! That's all. He's alone with . . . That's all. She goes. He's alone. That's all. If that ain't pain for real I burn my head. Mister Blues works me so hard. She goes. He's walking with the frost in his eyes, that's later, among the Korean hills, he gotta shave. It couldn't work he was afraid to tell her he'd do anything to keep her brown hand in his. The bald field cry in the morning. He is alone and his belly hurts he wanna sleep he don't wanna live he's alone I know it's wrong so what he's evil so what . . . . Nevermore baby that Blues so much I don't care if I die I say nevermore like that the Blues babe. Her walk vanishes among the stiff lines the gray, the branches, the night, though the sun already slides over the dead bodies of that shade. He's alone with the mean dawn. Crosswords. Bullshit. Legs and coats and shoes and canes and sticks. He's alone. ALONE! She goes. You ain't no good he thinks, ain't no room for you in here. He shouts. She goes. He's alone in a world he lived so much with, he's alone in the gray sidewalks the shops the houses the walls. This is so much; stiff fields under the heavy winter afternoon. Streamlets. Streams. Bullshit. Something has happened when she left. She leaves. She goes. He's alone there something happens ain't cold no more in there see you down there he means HELL he's running down along the road he wanna sleep ain't nothin else he can do babe you shouldn'ta left him alone. He dying you running. Fields. Hills. Bullshit.

Whipped down, the flood. It's cold now. Korea again. If he closes his eyes they all come, the old sick dogs, all them liars, and he shivers between the banks. The scene goes. There will be some night like that, falling down the ditch, harsh, harsh, harsh all over its weeds, just scraping the ground, just a high stinking of marsh, like a bunch of hungry crawlers. He stands up. He's alone in the very center of that land. He's alone. Dontyou cry! Dontyou yell! Just manage to die. GIT THE HELL OUTTA HERE MOTHERFUCKER! Just find yourself a place in that cold, just sit down and wait. 'T ain't gonna be long. Man! Say some'n! Do some'n! What's happenin here? Nothing. They all waiting. They caress the death hidden among the stones in the walls of their houses. They ain't doin nothing. They watch it come. Dig the shadow. Nothin. Waiting for they all frozen. Moveless for real. Dead for good.

Now the fear again. The smells. The silence. The matter was to live babe! Yeah that was the deal. The fire goes on, lightnin sometimes the thick walls, the scars in the walls. I'm alone. Something blows behind. . . . He sits down. All this is snow and rain, wordless. Who wanted to talk? Fuck. Burn. Take care, you could get down, all softened, slipping just like an evening, and wake up in a net of words. She was just a twelve year old Korean girl. When he took his hand off the dead body his fingers were stiff, he couldn't move his hand anymore. As though all his nerves were stuck to the moveless glance, as though she had swallowed up his life before dying. Nothin either. He ain't doin nothin. He just tries to move his fingers sometimes, but he knows he'll be dead before they wake up.

He could shake that whole frightened world with one big free laughter. But who's gonna be fresh enough to do it?

Endless dream. Endless dread. He ain't but a poor lonely figure and he thinks he thinks. Nigger they said. Run nigger run! You black drowned dream, you death! Looks like something wants to move there, all the days, the very old fears. . . . Damn this fucked up world! And they look at him, why ain't you with us, you think you different perhaps, you think you know better'n that. . . . You think your trouble's bigger'n ours, your love stronger? Men! Leave him alone he's a kid he won't grow up. . . . Turn me loose my song is with the sun. . . . Fuck you all! He wakes up with the sweat on his cheeks. Look at the flame don't think look. . . .

Blood and smile. Fields and paths and him, waking up, really awake now, he can feel every little blow, every breath in the air. Morning, young and stiff, and he doesn't want to think about his hunger. He looks around him. I feel white. Any white boy waking up in the morning must feel like that. And it's over. Already gone: he shouldn't have thought of it. The fear's back, and the dream, and the whole sickness of his days. It's like that every morning. Every morning for almost thirty years he's been waking up, knowing he didn't have but these three or four minutes to feel free, just three or four minutes to steal between the sleep and the dread. Now it's here. Wide, almost good in the stomach, good familiar taste of nightmare. Blood and smile.

He sees the cabin and the outhouse. It has to go fast. Some of his life is going to be played here. He doesn't know. It's the same everywhere. His life always happens where he is. Would he only stay there one second, it'd be as important. He just knows something is going to happen, something is happening right now. All of it has been too long, like lingering. He walks. Somebody is living there. He can hear his mother cursing: All them field niggers just ain't no good! He was a field nigger too. He looks at the house and thinks again: somebody is living there. He tries to think about this other life and it seems obscene, like every time he thinks about somebody as a person with feelings, love and anger, it seems obscene that all men wouldn't be rough pieces of dream and silent flesh. Somebody's living there. Kids grow up there, kids just like him get fucked up every day there, just like he did. He's almost arrived at the door now, but he's not in front of the house, nobody can see him. He walks a little faster, not knowing what he's going to say or do.

She comes out and stares at him without a word. He doesn't talk either. She grins and goes back in the house. She's a girl he thinks, and then, no, she's a woman. Dark, with a soft smile and a very young, very pure face, and an expression like a god slowly made into a devil by years of hopeless fight, with something like a deep cruelty. . . . He stays before the open door, motionless, he can hear her walking inside. She comes out and plunges her eyes into his.

"What you want?"

She's not that young he thinks. And right away: not that beautiful either.

"I wanna eat. . . ."

She started a crazy scared expression. Something like what he'd seen sometimes on white women's faces when they were suddenly in front of a Negro. . . . But she was no white woman. . . . That chick is nuts, he thought. I'd better go. She was looking at him with deep horror, and it lasted about twenty seconds. Then the smile came back.

"You can't come in," she said very softly.

Once more he wondered what was wrong with that woman. He whispered, you better git off that kick girl, but loud enough so she could hear it. Then he smiled at her and got closer.

"Listen sister, all I want is some'n to eat. . . ."

"Don't you git in!" She started yelling. "My husband ain't here, you can't come in."

He turned back and started walking. She called:
"Wait!"

He looked at her from where he was, without moving, and burst out in laughter.

"You just outta your mind babe. Better get yourself together!"

"Wait. . . . You not from here?" He didn't say a word. She seemed to be highly excited now. "You in trouble?"

He wanted to laugh. Shucks he thought. That gal is crazy. Then she had said "trouble" and he wanted to spank her for that. Beat something until he'd sit down and cry. Yeah, maybe he was in trouble. He walked back to her.

"Wutcha wanna do now?"

She seemed to look for an idea and said, as though she had just thought of it right then:

"Go hide in the shed. I'll bring you some."

He didn't answer and walked toward the shed. He knew she was looking at him, he could almost know her smile. He was terribly tired now. All the youth he had felt a few minutes ago was gone. The shed was just against the house, he could know what was happening inside by listening carefully. He was scared now. It was the first time for three weeks he was himself, not doing anything, just a burning bit of black fear. Maybe she was just scared because I'm dirty and my clothes are all torn up. She has no kids he thinks. She ain't thirty yet. Hunger was burning his stomach, he could hardly see. What the hell was she waiting for? Her man better come back soon he whispered. I don't want no bullshit with that woman.

It could be about eleven now. But he could not feel the morning anymore. Something was already rotten in this day, like very old. He thinks he should get high, it would make him feel better, just forget about how endless the fear is. He lies down on the hay, the whole shed is stinking, he thinks about that woman spending all her life in that stinking. No wonder she's mean. And yet he thinks: she's allright. All these people are allright. They might be the only ones to be allright now. . . . Loud and hard and true. But that there girl is all cracked up.

She comes in, silently, softly and he doesn't move. She sits at his side and he's still waiting, a ball of warm anguish moves in his belly, he can feel the dread getting near. He is stiff as a poplar trunk he is afraid to move, he knows whatever he'll do will break it up. She looks at him, her face close to his and she talks, she starts talking all alone, as though she didn't care about his hearing or not.

"You tired. . . . You don't know. . . . He ain't bad but he just don't want nobody around." She was slowly nodding her head, as if she was about to cry, just like a little girl. She kept on. . . . "He done wounded a man last year, just for nothin." She was almost crying now. . . . "But you know he ain't bad. . . ."

He looked at her, wondering whether she was playing or not. Something in him prevented him from participating. She didn't seem to care.

"All I wants is kids. But he dont wanna have none. He makes me stay home all day and he dont want me to go to town. You know it's all because he ain't black. . . ."

He flips. He got up, ready to leave; he thought; something had told me this was a trick. . . .

"You mean . . . Your husband is WHITE?"

"No, no. . . . He nigger alright. . . ."

"What you mean then, he ain't black?"

"It's because he light, just like a white man. . . ." He thought: now she's going to cry again. . . . She looked at him with shining eyes and he felt his whole body tightening. His hunger was slowly getting displaced into his mind, images were passing through his head and it seemed just natural that he would be blind to the present. His arm went to touch her breast under the greasy dress. She didn't move. He let his hand wrap up the flesh and she was looking at him while he was sitting down again, her eyes seeming to say: I dare you to do it! I dare you to touch me again. . . .

The blood beats in him. He gets up again and shouts.

"Git out!"

She gets up too, and lets her hands hang to his while her head falls against his chest. She is gonna cry again he thinks. I don't wanna hear no crying. He drives her back.

"Don't start crying now! I'm goin. . . ."

And right away he's beating her, beating her hard, slow swinging blows in the face and he can hear a soft sound of crying in between.

She was still almost motionless, just her head was swinging from left to right at every blow. He stopped,

62

knowing that it wouldn't help, his rage was somewhere else, he hadda live with it all way long. Right away he knew beating her wouldn't change, couldn't change anything. All of it seemed to be written in advance, as though he didn't have nothing to decide, just play the part. He knew he had to keep his anger, feed it like a baby, until he could throw it to the sons of bitches who deserve it. But the temptation had been too strong to get rid of it before, just now. . . . They both lay down, she was still sobbing silently, he took her face into his hands and caressed it with a slow, nearly mechanical motion. He stared at the convulsive lips, the deep hatred in her eyes and once again he stiffened, knowing he desired this face and this body, not knowing how to stop his beating blood. She let him undress her and he was blind, she had to help him twice, the shed seemed to have become dark. . . . It's probably hunger he thought, and suddenly he remembered the peck's face, in the Club, and how he had hit the fat chin, and he looked at her with tenderness. She got it and asked:

"What's the matter now?"

"Nothin baby. . . . You're nice. . . . I didn't wanna beat you."

"When Lester come back he kill you. . . . I tell him. . . . You see, ahma tell him and he kill you. . . ."

He didn't answer and looked at her naked body. SHE'S BLACK he thought. SHE'S BLACK. He had still the cracker's face in his eyes, it was good to remember his

**63**

falling down at his knees, every time I feel bad he thought, I'll remember him and everything will be allright. He felt new again, like when he had wakened up this morning. He suddenly felt the need to talk to her, to tell her about the fear, and the dream, and the bastard in the Club. . . . He bowed his head over her mouth and she thought he was going to kiss her. She tried to avoid the kiss but he didn't move. Why couldn't he talk to her? Why couldn't he talk to anybody? SHE'S BLACK he thought again. And right away he wanted to laugh. HE WAS BLACK TOO. Both of'em were black but he was still thinking about it. She got her head up.

"Why you laughin?"

"Nothin. . . . I was thinking of some'n that's funny. . . ."

He couldn't help it. He was laughing inside: no white stupid ass would think he is fucking a WHITE bitch if he does. . . . But he hadda remember that girl is black. He knew the anger was coming back. For years it had been the same hopeless hide and seek with rage. . . . She looked at him and he knew that now, SHE was scared.

"What kind o' trouble you got?"

"I hit someone. . . ."

"You ain't gotten in no mess with white folks is you?"

He hadda tell her. He hadda tell somebody.

"Yeah. . . . I done told you. I hit a cracker." He was

64

feeling tired now. Maybe it would be better that they'd come and get him now. She looked horrified.

"They knows you's here?"

"No baby, don't be scared. They don't know. They ain't even lookin for me."

He suddenly realized that. They were not even looking for him. In other words he was free. But he was still frozen, he was like an old man, something's broken in him, he can live allright but he just doesn't feel like it and at the same time he hangs on to it, every day he wants to live some more. He gave her a look, remembering they were both naked, and he thought again: black girl. He took her in his arms and he could feel that she was breathing aloud and fast, he could feel how alive she was. Maybe she was . . . Maybe she could warm me up a little. He started to kiss her all over the body and he took her and she was weakly moving like someone being drowned and he knew he was hurting her but he couldn't stop. She was biting her lips and he sucked the blood, just the same taste as his when he had sucked his fingers the day before, or before, he didn't remember. . . . Then he was calm. That was taken. Put apart. Whatever would happen now that had become part of him, wouldn't nobody take it back.

"What's your name?"

"Why you wanna know now?"

She looked angry again. Why the hell couldn't he

understand people? He was already far . . . her voice was calling him back:

"Why you wanna know now? You didn't care before! You just didn't want to know none, just beat me and . . . "

She didn't want to say it. She's a girl he thinks. Indeed. She couldn't be but a girl. I never met no woman. Just girls. She bows the head and says:

"I'm Pearl. . . ."

"I'm . . . " He wanted to say "sorry" but he felt how ridiculous it would have been. He was trying to imagine her life, the millions of lives like hers, and he thought of his mother again. He hadn't thought of his mother for years and it was the second time today.

"Too bad Lester he goin kill you . . . I like you allright."

He wondered if she was kidding.

"You gonna tell him?"

"Sure. He ain't no killer. . . . He workin all day and here comes a no-good nigger take his wife. Lawd! He ain't no killer but sure as hell he gointer kill you!"

"Why you done it then?"

"I ain't done nothin!"

"When he come back?"

"You better git outta here right now!"

She was already up and dressed. She looked at him with the same expression of challenge she'd had before.

"Wutcha waitin for? Git goin!"

"I wanna eat."

"Wait."

She ran out and he started to get dressed, slowly. He wasn't afraid of her husband coming back. All of that didn't really matter. . . . The real life was somewhere else, somewhere else the real world. . . . What the hell did all this mean? Didn't nobody on this side have the power on his own life . . . Gestures, words, empty . . . They could come and get him, Lester could come and kill him, he could die, or live, or just vanish, what would be the difference? Black lives just mean nothing. . . . They happen in a closed circle and can't get out of it, no matter how much they move, no matter what they do. She was coming back with the food. A plate of rice, and fruit. He started eating with his hands.

"Your Lester . . . When he comin back?"

"Never mind. He be back soon enough! eat!"

"I wanted to tell you . . . "

She looked at him and he wondered whether he'd be able to tell her.

"I just want you to remember me. . . . Not because of that . . . but just because I was tryna do some'n . . . somethin for us."

"Hittin the white man?"

"Yeah maybe. . . . "

He could see the anger coming back in her eyes.

"You wasn't doin nothin fer us. You jes' hit'im cause you wanted to. . . . You wasn't doin none. . . . Wutcha

**67**

think? You think you's some black leader now? If you so great why ain't you goin beat two or three thousand of'em? Sure that would do some. . . . But you ain't but a chicken. . . . Lester he comin back and you see what a man is. . . . Great Gawd Awmighty! See that nigger there, thinks he some'n else jes' cause he done scratched the man's nose! I'm tellin you, that ain't got nuttin-a-do with me. . . . "

Suddenly he wanted to run. Get away from that voice. . . . He finished eating and got up.

"Too bad babe. . . . You and me couldda gotten along fine!"

"Git the hell outta here! You and me? You sure's crazy!"

He didn't answer. He started to walk out slowly and he knew she was walking out with him. Once out she stopped and he kept on walking toward the road and she was yelling:

"Hey! Preacher! You jes' don't have to tell me good-bye! You jes' meet Lester and give him the message!"

He was walking. It had all started again. The run-away to nowhere, the fear, the road and his life let among the brambles in bits of bleeding flesh. Already he had almost forgotten Pearl, and the cabin and her naked black breasts in the shed. He was going ahead, blind, dirty stinking black figure moving in the corn.

*

*     *

This was the town. Something was to be done here. He looked at the roofs extended under his eyes, like a wide flat gray land of iron and wood and tiles. A city. It seems that his life has become a long lonesome walk, and he can't stop anywhere. People can die and love, he's already gone while they still look for their way in dark sheds. And he knows this too: he envies them. He hasn't ever been able to find himself a shed where he'd stay, for which he'd fight and bleed. A city. People there know why they die, know why they're being killed, why they want to live. Every day his anger looks emptier; he remembers a time when he had known, everything was simple, all white folks just had to be killed and everything would be straight. . . . Then he'd started to think that all men should get along, he wanted to call every white man he'd meet brother! But soon he'd found out that white men don't want no black brothers. They want boys. That had been crap again. No brother. And now he could feel his hatred ready to burst, but he didn't know whom he hated, he didn't know what he was mad at anymore. Bullshit. No wonder this here world is fucked up. A city. He'd go through that city and his passing wouldn't change nothing. He'd talk and eat and smile and fight again, and this city would keep closed to him, just because he was from nowhere, just because he wasn't able to love it. . . . The world was not fucked up: he was.

He had been back home very late. Gloria had left for Chicago the next morning. He didn't want to think she had done it just because she was leaving. But he thought it was a little unjust that she should leave right after that, he would have no time to make it last a little.

That was just continuing. The road and his memory slowly unrolling along the hedges. He walks and once more he's not there. The same long roll of images: Gloria, Maurice, Korea, and thousands of howling faces, of distorted smiles, fire and blood, and the same old taste of fear like a familiar bullet of cotton in the stomach, and he can feel it in his throat sometimes, when it comes up. Sour and hot.

There had been days and nights, rumor and soft silence. His drunkenness in the dark dawn, walking. And he knew he was crossing the bullshit again. Just because he didn't want to get hung on a place where he'd know people, have habits, a place to stay, with a work and a time to be there. Just because he wanted to believe that he wouldn't stand it, he would have to split and fuck it all. Just because he wouldda liked to think that he had not chosen, that his walking with silence and vacuum in his life all way along the same lonesome groove was HIS way, as if he hadn't done anything to get there, foreigner all the time, outsider for real. And confusedly he knew that was just *too* nice, it sounded too literary, some of it had to be false. False and obscene.

Such a waste of freedom! Folks fight sweat and bleed to get a tenth of his freedom and they'll probably never get it. He had gotten it but he wouldn't use it. Something like a buried laughter seemed to come up and die on his lips. If I met a cat like me I'd probably hate his guts!

A city. He suffered from being out of its life and passion, out of its bloodshot stream, and the mere idea that he might get hooked in people and times and places scared him to death, made him sick. But something was telling him that this had to be the real life. That the real world was among the day-to-day chattering, a world of salaries and housing and solidarity and civil rights and serious people. He would have, if he wanted to give up his fucked up hopes of being nowhere, he would have to love that, love it all the way. Share the same future, no matter how foolish it could seem, the same hatreds, however senseless they would look. Love it. Meet brothers and love them, or hate them, but talk to them, grant them that much life, and start to love their voices their gestures their warmth, his own voice his own gestures; and learn how to walk in that world with a smile of recognition and brotherhood, and learn how to get something out of his anger and hatred, instead of wasting them in senseless shots. And the wide feeling of rest he'd get out of being in a world that words can't reach, can't wreck. Yeah, he reckoned that was the deal, the real matter: be somewhere that words just can't touch or attain; be naturally justified by hunger or sexual obsession, by murder or satisfaction. And all he had was fear and hatred, unsharable.

Gloria . . .

He started to walk a little faster. It could be about one now. The rice he'd eaten started to weigh, heavy on his stomach, and the hunger was coming back. He thought: I gotta shave. At least I gotta shave. And wash too. Folks gonna think I'm hoboin!

She'd left in the morning. He'd told his mother he was goin'a fish with Tom and some other boys, and he'd gone to the station with her. Sure as hell I'm goin'a be 'lone. And it was like accepting it, like already being on the other side of her leaving. He had felt her surprise. With a little bitterness he'd thought: maybe she was glad 'cause she thought I was goin to cry. And he was slightly ashamed to think that. She kissed him. Lawd have 'mercy he thought, she's goin! His head started to beat crazily, as if he was looking for some way to prevent her from going. I'll write to you she said. And he had the feeling that he was older than her. Just because she missed so much pride, just because she couldn't hide that she was suffering, just because he knew he loved her much more than she would ever love him and he didn't cry.

He sits down on the slope. The road is going down, he's almost arrived in town. He feels a terrible will to be clean, sharp. Like when he was in school and his pants were always too big, he hadda hold'em back with a belt, a string, or anything, and he'd let the shirt cover them, so it wouldn't show. And he never wanted to take the shirt off, or even to open it, because one wouldda seen the pants and the belt, the pants going up to his chest and the belt cutting them in the middle. It has been like that for years, he'd never had pants of his size. He might have been fourteen or fifteen the first time he'd had pants that would really fit him.

That's a long time he hasn't been in a city. Almost a month. The trouble with places is that after a while, if you know a lot of places, you get'em all mixed up in your mind. He was like that. He couldn't, he really couldn't feel the same impression of strange and new he'd felt the first time he'd moved to another country. It seemed that everything, even the air he breathed was different. But now all that was over. Everywhere he felt the same. Home. Or nowhere. *Just because he'd been to so many places and he didn't want to belong to none of 'em.*

He is still sitting on the slope. He looks around him and breathes the hot dust. *Just because he didn't want to belong to none of 'em.* The town seems to challenge him now. *Just because he didn't want to belong nowhere.* Fields fields fields and roads and cabins and the blues in every groove. *To belong nowhere.* Something in him is just getting ready to be born. *To belong nowhere.* He smiles and it's like he's sharing a big joke with that ground. *Nowhere* . . . Yeah! Yeah, here he belonged! He gets up suddenly. He's there standing up in the middle of the road, he can hear the many rumors of a country town before him, and it's as though something had struck him all of a sudden, hard deep blow on his life. Nothing has happened, he's been there walking for three days, he's alone and nothing has happened but he starts to see it all now, the sickness and his run, and he starts to understand, and he's scared to see it all. Here he belongs. No, he couldn't take it: here he belonged. And that he'd just understand it now, that he would only find it out now, just like that. And immediately he wants to laugh. It can't be true. And he also knows it is true. But he keeps trying to escape it. Something that happens within a man's mind just can't be true. Maybe nothing of it is really true. Looking for a way out. It comes back and it's like a whole new life unfolds, above him. He was home. That sure was good to know. Maybe that was it. His legs can hardly bear him, he shivers as though his whole life was being played here, in two minutes. Maybe all his trouble was just coming from that: he was home and he didn't know. Or he didn't want to know. He sits down again, the jubilation of the first minute is going, he gotta think about it. He remembers the chick's face. Pearl. That chick was right to treat me as though I was a foreigner. I was. A smile pulls his lips and he doesn't even know it. He imagines what kind of life he'll be able to have if he accepts it, if he agrees with it, if he accepts to believe it. If I really make myself at home, 't could be great. But he's a kid. He's gotta learn how to live here. Again he laughs. Ain't that a bitch? He's been all over the world and he hadn't been able to escape race. His color had been filling up his mind for years, he hadn't ever been able to think about anything else and it was the first time in years that he'd found back the same freedom he had as a kid, with love and laughter. . . . He'd had to come back down here in Mississippi to find it. For years he hadn't thought of nothing but race and here, just because it was obvious in every furrow, on every field that the whole land was black, here he could afford to remember Gloria otherwise than as a black chick. He started to walk down toward the city with the same feeling of nervous joy as a kid who's about to show a new toy to his buddies. If only I can keep it. If I know how to use it. He was not afraid. He was going to walk in his life with it, and he'd get along. He knew it couldn't have happened just like that, it had to have been a long underground work in him. And now here it was, straight and loud. Years and years he'd been looking for a colorless and translucid humanity, just because he didn't want to be black, because he'd believed it when he'd been told that it was bad to be black. And it was like magic. He just had to say: I'm black and it's good. And right away he'd laugh and be strong. Forever. He'd whisper the words and wouldn't nobody, nothing ever be in a position to hurt him. He'd be as secure as he felt remembering the peck's face when he had hit him. I'm black and it's good. That was the new toy. I'm black and it's good. I'm black and it's good I'm black and . . . He was repeating the words as if it were a magic formula. I'm black and it's good. He hurried up, wanting to be in town, to meet people. I gotta tell'em. If we could know that! All of us! Lord how strong we'd be! Know it and sing it loud: we're black and it's good! If I could ever tell'em all no white trash on earth would ever be able to hurt any of us. If I can remember it, hold it back and remember it whatever happens, whatever they do to me, if I can they won't touch me. Never. Because I won't agree, because I will know, really know they're wrong, and sick, and fucked up, and rotten motherfuckers. Not because they do it to me. But because I know I'm black and it's good.

He's in town now. He's gotten there by the right side. The black belt. He can see the faces around him, tall black figures, and kids running around him. He was having a weird feeling, like very naive, the kind of feeling at which he would have laughed before: they were his people. Funny. He used to think he was beyond that, over it. In fact, he wasn't there yet. Wan't that something else? He used to feel that he knew much better'n to love black folks just because he was a boot himself. And now he was finding out that it required much more courage, that he hadn't been big enough to do it. There was a whole new world opened before his eyes and it all depended on him that he'd really get into it, and live with it. All, the mere gestures, the words and the people, everything would take a new face. And he also knew that it had been coming for a long time, that he had always known there would be a day that he wouldn't be able to escape anymore. That day had come. What he was going to do with it, what he was going to live was still a dark backwater waiting for stream. And he hadda invent it all. But it was almost like having found back a faith, a new strength, a youth. Sure he was gonna live.

It ain't such a big thing after all, is it? No one can really tell where it starts, or how. But the time comes when one wonders whether it's all that important. And then you go on, tell your little story, your little fairy tale; in fact nothing has changed, chickens are still sticking to their borders. Life has to be there or here, if it ain't right it's all wrong, don't you get out of history's stream, transitional types have to die—but Lawd have a mercy I'm just one of 'em—burn your ass for your grandson and whatever happens don't forget to roam, complain, and pretend you might be heard. They say that's the way it works. I don't mind. I haven't got any choice anyway. . . . But this is supposed to be protest literature. Don't mess too much with the truth, nobody cares about it, and your enemies might find something there. Don't you fuck around telling the truth man! You here to convince, you dig? What you come here talking about reality for? What you trying to do man? Act against us? You just sellin out, that's what!

Okay. I ain't goin'a give you no truth. I'm so fuckin hip that parties don't make that scene. But they goof. They wrong. Them horribly clean lies ain't nothin next to the truth. But they clean. Reality ain't. It's just so horrible anybody can dig it. 'T belongs to everybody. That's also why none of 'em want it. The Truth! Ladies and Gentlemen won't you buy a little bit of truth? 25 cents of truth? Just a tiny loaf of truth to take back home to your ol' lady, to your sweet man, to your big fat mama, to your ugly boyfriend . . . 25 cents of truth ladies and gentlemen to grow in a pot on the street corner's queer's window. . . . C'mon there is enough for everybody truth ain't that precious nowadays but it's a sweet cereal that will recall you the old times, come on ladies and gentlemen 25 cents of truth it's a good bargain and my truth ladies and gentlemen ain't no bullshit, it's first choice, it's not political, it don't even think, don't you wanna take some of my dumb truth home? . . . Lord they don't even want it, what the hell am I gonna do with all that stuff, the fuzz better not catch me with it. . . . Ha! Ha! Ha! . . . Whutyou doin here boy? I see you blowin. . . . You gettin high. . . . Lemme smell. . . . Well boy you good for the chair! Hey marshal! That nigger there he smokin truth. . . . Put his ass in jail!

The very thing is that the faithful ones don't understand it and the smart ones don't want to ever admit it. A drag all way long. But this is the way the book's got to be written: it's the only sane way, it's a matter of mental safety, emotional balance. Only the truth, but not all the truth. Like this cat Daniel Peebles, he'd had a real rough time all his life, a real victim, one would say. Okay. Yet I swear the Lord there must have been something very naturally healthy about him. Or very naturally capable of getting along with insanity. Great God. Things ain't that simple either. . . .

Then we can go on with the story. First it must be pathetic. Only pathos makes good-sellers. 'T must be serious too. If not it's a betrayal. Get dumb man! Blow!

But don't you ever forget this, reader: it ain't but a novel. You can't cry too much over it. All that was born in my head. And my man Peebles he ain't no hero; you can't stick to him and suffer with him and cry over your fuckin self. Cause you white. He ain't. You're not being cursed out and beaten up and spat upon. If you're somebody in this story, you're that good-open-minded-natural-cracker. If you were not you wouldn't be reading this. But this is why I broke the story a while to talk to you: what comes next might be bloody. And it ain't but a novel; it ain't but a story that was born in my head. Don't forget it. And remember you are not the one who bleeds. In the story as well as anywhere else. If you keep that in mind I can go on with the story. The mere fact it could be born in my head is scaring enough ain't it? For that story, that particular one may be false, but the reason why you keep reading is you know it might be true, you know if it hadn't happened some day somewhere just like that I couldn't have invented it.

But what about him? That Peebles son-of-a-gun. . . . What if the reality of his life was lying somewhere else. What if he had accepted, I don't mean dispossession, I don't mean some cracker's insane motives, but just that THAT was where he had to start from, in order to go anywhere else, not trying to catch up with no train, but just incapable of seeing any link between that story and the words folks would put upon it, the words anybody would name it, incapable of seeing any link between that story and what he'd actually been living.

Go on. . . . Call it alienation, call it estrangement. . . . Your whole language is a whole lotta bullshit. That's what it would have been for YOU, if YOU were put there all of a sudden. But why would you understand it? No matter how you try: you're not ever gonna understand it, unless you already KNOW! Now keep out of it. All you can do is take it. Just like that. Just accept this truth: what you don't understand can also exist, all that your brain can't take is not necessarily false. Take it as a whole. Don't be sorry feeling that your efforts to level, your efforts to resemble are being made vain. You just go ahead and take it like that, just the way it is. If you can do that you've done far more than you ever dreamt of!

Actually a whole lotta things don't fit with the very precise drag one is supposed to talk about. The very same problems in fact, but requiring entirely DIFFERENT answers. And that's what bugs one, actually, that the more you know about universality the more acutely you feel the need and the reality of that which is un-takable, of what's peculiar. Simply that if you don't already know it ain't no point tryin'a understand because it really ain't got nothin to do with words and lines and thoughts, since everything there is just a deal with some inner bullshit. And it's funny. And it's somehow laughable, that need to put it down on paper with the whole crappy emotional equipment, Psychoanalysis and Co. Maybe it's all a matter of sex and ass. . . . And yet it takes place: it's the very unacceptable fact: it did happen just like that, it shouldn't be but what the feats were. . . . The gas, the big motherfuckin joke is that everyone knows, but it would break their plans. Then they keep messing around with the same rotten meaningless words, and they claim that's life, and I wake up and say: if that's life it ain't worth a dime, and I go kill my fuckin self just because I believed them. . . .

Listen, reader: all that ain't nothing but me calling you back down to earth. I saw you were ready to fly all the way up with my man Peebles. . . . But don't. . . . That's not your job. . . . You here to read. . . . Not to become somebody else. . . . If you want to change you change when you're over with the book . . . you'll have chances to change, don't worry. But right now you stay down here with me, on the level of this page, and let Peebles go. . . .

He walks into the bar. Dead glances, rhythmless figures. He looks around him, stunned, as though he had never seen such a bar, never seen these people. A big fat man walks to him, and he stares at the sweaty face with a kind of distrust, like he can't believe what he is seeing. The thick body swings toward him. Something like a big roar gets out.

"Wutcha want, my man?"

He thinks: that cat probably believes I'm beggin or some. . . . Hope he'll give me a room.

Easy man, easy. . . . He was thinking very slowly, very cautiously, not wanting to start on a wrong track. He was looking for some story he could tell the man, but his mind was empty, he was like coming out of a

**87**

long sleep. I'll have to get used to living again, he thought.

"You got a room for me?" He's incapable of not telling the truth. . . . It's a weird feeling, he'll also have to get used to lying again. He plunges his eyes into the man's and he can feel a wall of hostility tumbling down, as if the man's resistance were melting away.

"Depends. . . ." He could see the man wanted to be nice, but didn't want to show it. . . . "You got some money?"

"No, but I'll get some. . . ."

"Listen buddy, I don't know how you gonna git that loot, and I mean not to know. But I just don't want no kind o' trouble nohow. Dug?"

"It's allright with me. You ain't gonna have no trouble. I'm straight." He thought: why the fuck do we have to go through all that bullshit? We both know he'll give me the room anyway. But he knew it couldn't happen otherwise.

The man took him upstairs and gave him a big hand to shake. The warm roar sounded again.

"They call me Richie. But my real name is Napoleon. I ain't been here a year. I'm from Louisiana. New Orleans. Ever been there?"

"No." He too wanted to be nice, but he was awkward. He didn't know how to start. He smiled at the man and said, "My name is Dan. Dan Peebles. You know . . . You don't have to give me that room man, I mean, if you think I ain't goin'a pay you or some, or I'm a hustler. . . ."

"You nuts fella! Go on and git some sleep!"

Napoleon-Richie opened the door, let the key on the lock, pushed him in and walked back down the stairs with a calm laughter. He was amused. There was a kind of tenderness in his roaring.

The room was small, dark. He put the light on, and the lamp was weak, a kind of dusty yellow light. He walked to the broken mirror over the sink and looked at his dirty unshaven face with amazement. That was him allright. I'll wash later, he thought. He took off his shoes, his feet started stinking, he walked to the window, gave a look at the yard, silent, and the garbage cans. He walked back to the bed. Two steps. That was a small room allright. He lay down. Lay down. Life was simple. . . . Really simple, that was the truth. Simple. He lay down. A bed. He lay down on the bed, simply. He didn't have to sleep. Just simply lay down on that bed.

It's a too long dream. Too far a thought. Something that comes back up, back from the past, like shining. He lay down on the bed. Back from that very simple past. There was a new world unfolding before his eyes, he had thought. And maybe that was it. Something back from the past on the edge of which he would have to live. Learn how to breathe.

That cat in New York . . . Funny he'd remember him! So long ago! Doudou. They called him Doudou. Tall strong fellow with a funny hat. Doudou. Funny cat.

He was there. Life is simple. There he was, lying on that bed as if it were natural. I should have done it before. Just walk in the place and ask for a room and tell the man I'm broke but it won't last and lie down on a bed and see how marvelous and simple life is. He can feel his head sinking into the pillow. Lord it's good! No fear. Anguish made warm, made blanket. Doudou sure was a funny sonofagun, talkin that shit all the time. No dread. Warm, warm. Anguish made familiar made gentle. No, I don't think Doudou was really his name. That was just like when they'd called him Abdul, in Europe, because he was always hangin around with Arabs. Warm blanket and it wraps up his body, just letting his head out. Doudou was crazy, why the hell am I thinking about that motherfucker now? Warm. He sleeps.

Jazz. There was Jazz flowing up from the yard. Sounded like Bird. Maybe Sonny Stitt. Warm, good. That was Bird, sure that was Bird. Warm dread in him too. How the world could that man put dread in music?

The record was old, scratching. Good. Good. He goes back to sleep. Bird. Doudou. Simple life.

He wakes up suddenly. Sweating. It was a nightmare, but he can't remember what it was. Crazy how fast memory makes it. The house is full of noise. Music, voices. Many voices downstairs, at the bar. What time is it? I don't give a damn. He sits down. Wash. He gotta wash. Back down here in Mississippi, down home. So many years. His life is empty. It's a shame such an empty life, and it's gonna remain like that, I won't ever do anything outta my life. There must be something rotten in the way I grew up. He burst out into laughter: something rotten in the way twenty million kids grew up!

He remembers Doudou. One day they were walking, it was somewhere in Brooklyn, there was nobody but an old white man, not really old, but like half-dead, no light in his eyes. They had passed by him, he was standing up in the middle of the sidewalk, it was about eleven o'clock at night, and the man's voice had risen, shy, obscene.

"Excuse me, sir, have you got a light?"

Doudou looked at him, stiff and silent.

"Sir?" The man was like begging. Doudou grinned. He looks at the man, and the words fall out of his mouth, dry.

"Poor white trash!"

The man hasn't heard. Or pretends he hasn't heard. He keeps waiting there, disgusting with defeat. Then Doudou gets his good dancer's leg up, a terribly quiet smile widens and tears his face, and suddenly he throws his shoe, a big blow of the heel into the man's face. The guy falls down on the ground, gets up and runs away, terrified. Doudou's face hasn't moved at all while he hit. His smile gets fluid, cool. He starts walking again. He had looked at him. Doudou had stood his look and whispered:

"I am a nigger!"

He gets up and walks to the sink. Empty fuckin life. How can Doudou live? Why doesn't he get killed, acting the way he does, all the time? There must be a science. I wish I knew. He plunges his feet into the water, thinking: I am nobody. I am a fucking nobody. If I died now wouldn't nobody mind, wouldn't nobody even know. He dries his foot with the brown towel and starts washing the other one with his hand. It's night. Downstairs the voices get louder, he can hear Richie's laughter's big roar among the noise. Fat warm man. Anybody. There was a violence he wants to find back. A heat, something like blood and calm hatred. Nothing he'd find with Richie. That was dangerous: this blanket of warm anguish, this happiness. He dries the second foot, runs down some more water and puts his face in the sink. He can feel the dirt, the blood, all that in bites and edges in his beard, melting in the water between his fingers. It would be good to be clean. Real clean. The water runs into his nostrils, it's fresh, it scrapes his throat. That sure violence! Why Doudou? Look for it. Look for it day and night.

He walks down the stairs, walks between the people and sits down behind a table. Richie's big hand falls on his shoulder and he flips. That gesture! . . . Then they both laugh and the man sits down in front of him, there is nothing alarming in his smile. Everything is warm and quiet about him. Once again he shivers, thinking, that happiness is frightening. Richie keeps watching him, smiling. He doesn't know what to do. Something in his mind is saying: this nigger is dangerous. . . . Fuckin Uncle Tom makin believe he happy like mad . . . Right away he is ashamed: that man ain't no Uncle Tom, he's just cool. Ain't no white folks around right now, why would he be mad? Lord, I'm so sick he whispers slowly. Richie's laughter bursts out again.

"Right fella, we's all sick. But no sweat, some'n will happen, some day. . . . We's sick allright, you know, but it's not natural. Somethin happened that made us sick. Don't know what. Some'n that happened long ago. Git it?"

"Yeah. . . ."

He was thinking: is it possible that he doesn't know the name of that which happened? Is he an idiot, or a sage?

93

"Where you from?" There was this persistent softness in his big voice.

"Right here in Mississippi. 'Bout forty miles from here."

"Comin back home, huh?"

"Hmm hmm, that's how you can call it."

The man looked at him intently and spoke again.

"Don't let them rob it man."

"WHAT?"

"I say don't let *them* rob it." He was smiling, still quiet, as though they were a pair of lovers too happy to say a word.

"But . . . let them rob what?"

"Your life man! Don't let them steal away your goddam life. Bug 'em to death, hav 'em kiss your ass, but don't let them steal it. It's YOURS brother, yours and no one else's! All you can do is live."

"No." His voice was cold now. Good, he'd found back his way. "No." He mentally thanked the man for having helped him to find it back. "No man, that's not what I can do."

"What you think you gonna change, gittin your ass lynched? Young man, young fellow . . . What you think you can do? I'm tellin you, somethin happened that must be undone, but by who? You ain't big 'nuff! Don't let 'em lynch your ass nigger, don't give it to them!"

He thought Richie, oh Richie! Why is it? Why you and me and them around me and them that walk like shadows all around our own shades? And he thought of Doudou again. Was it the way? He felt a need to go out. He smiled at Richie and said:

"I gotta go out. Tomorrow I'll start lookin for a job. Can you lay a dollar on me?"

"The way you seem to be going it's probably a bad investment, ace, but here! . . ."

He took the bill, put it into his pocket, shook the big hand and got out.

The street was noisy, voices and music and all, and heat and quarrels and fever and music again and noise, noise, noise. He felt the dread over the street like a mean sheet of sickness and earthy, dusty tan over a too slim face. Look for that very violence beyond this dead curtain of dream and fear. How? He was losing himself in the walk, like being ceaselessly about to be drowned. How would he find back Doudou in that crowded mud? And why? He had slept. Yesterday was longgone. He remembered: I'm black and it's good, and he laughed. How could he be so ridiculous? He looked at the street, thousands of messed up kids and phony preachers and happy cadavers and sick killers and crazy bitches and holy sisters and everyone getting high and laughing his head off and where the fuck would he find a hole in that crowd where he'd have Doudou grow up and spring and swing. . . .

Shit! He spat on the ground. Why do twenty million people, idiots and geniuses included, have to lead a tragic life? It don't make sense. A tragic life for twenty million women, kids and men who otherwise wouldn't want nothing but a little pot and a little pussy. . . . And here I am, looking for the spirit of a crazy sonofabitch who probably died long ago, 'cause don't nobody live long the way he did!

It was a long story. Years, and he had never known what he was looking for. How can a man be black? How could one live with it, as though it were an irrelevant detail, how could one not see? I'm sick. Maybe that's what it just means. Maybe sickness is the only way a spook can live? But was Doudou sick? Doudou didn't hate. He had seen his quiet face several times in his memory, the quietness of his face when he had thumped the man, the quietness of his voice when he had said: I am a nigger. He had envied that calm strength.

Back. The fear is back allright. He gotta do something so he can forget about it. That's his whole life: look for it, then get rid of it; look for it again and forget it; look for it and forget it. Endless circle. His walk recovers its swinging softness. It's back. Shit! To be all by myself, lonely as hell in the midst of a town, that's a shame. He suddenly becomes aware of the people around him, hard-faced men and young chicks with lipstick messing their faces. He walks, waving at everyone he crosses. They answer, waving back, and it's like a game, or getting back into a church where everybody knows you, because you're the nephew of the brother who works with the younger son of the Reverend's cousin. It's crazy, he thinks, these people wave at anybody they see! . . . Or maybe they think they know me, but they guess they've forgotten who I am and they don't want to be impolite or something like that. I'd like to know how far it can go. . . . He laughed inside. Maybe I could jump at a woman and start kissing her on the cheeks calling her auntie and she'd think she knows me and take me home for dinner. . . . Shit, he whispered, that's no way of communicating with folks, keep lookin at 'em like I am a Martian and I don't know nothin about how they live and all that crap!

He noticed a girl sitting on a stone against the wall of a bar. There was music coming out of the open door, and more voices. A whole rhythmic sound pushing its waves out of the room, horn and words and laughter and anger mixed up. He stops in front of the chick. She's nice. Not really beautiful, not really good-lookin face, but breasts, hips and ass, all very cool, swinging, exciting and real. He sits down at her side. She doesn't move. He doesn't look at her, his head turned toward the street, and his voice sounds good on that canvas of noise and sound.

"You got somethin to smoke?"

She hands him a cigarette out of a pack. He doesn't take it and looks at her.

"I mean to SMOKE!"

She laughs.

"Wutcha tryin'a do babe? Git me into trouble? I just don't know what you talkin 'bout."

He smiled, like forcedly.

"Okay, baby sister. I can't tell you anything. That's your right."

He kept sitting there, motionless. It was stupid, but he'd been hurt because the girl had thought he might be a cop or some kind of pigeon. I shouldn't let that kind of bullshit bother me. That's nothin. Just a chick that don't want to turn me on. That's nothin. The girl looks at him.

"Okay, I reckon I'm a fool, 'cause I ain't ever seen you 'round, but you look straight. C'mon!"

They got up and he followed her down the street. She turned at a corner and sat down again on the sidewalk, in a short street with no light. He kept standing up in front of her.

"Sit down baby. What's your name?"

"Daniel. Daniel Peebles."

"Awright Dan. Mine's Mary, ain't that sweet? It sure is a bad fittin name for me, but I ain't got none else, and I'm pretty lucky I got one, 'cause I might be called G.W. or some shit like that. . . . You got skins?"

"I ain't got nothin."

"Man, you're a drag, I don't know why I keep wastin my time with you anyway. Here!" She got some paper out of her pocket. She had a bloodlike red dress with two large pockets. She handed him the paper.

"Can you roll?"

He took the paper, she put the marijuana in it, out of a small leather bag that she put back in her pocket. He rolled a thin cigarette, slowly, it was funny, the gestures were like a rite, it all belonged to the same stoned world. Lord! he liked that! It was like getting back in a room outta which he'd been thrown. Yeah, it was good accomplishing the same slow gestures, rolling the pot between the fingers, sucking the edge of the paper, twisting the tip. Good. He looked at the chick and his eyes were like begging.

"Let's roll another one right now!"

She stares at him, and smiles.

"Lawd have a mercy, man, you fresh! You know what you want. I buy that shit man, I don't mean to give it away to the first no-good nigger that come around!" She laughed, there was no anger in her voice, just she was having a ball. "Okay," she said. "Roll another joint, but there ain't gonna be no third one, I swear the Lord!"

She got the leather bag out of her pocket and he started the same slow gestures. Good, yeah, it was good to roll a joint like that. Just the unlighted street and the sweet night and that funny chick turning me on. He finished doing the stick and kept the other one in his left hand. He put it in his mouth. She lighted a match and he burned the tip. He breathed the smoke, profoundly. Good, good. Lord, that was so good. He breathed again and he knew it would be good because he hadn't eaten and he breathed again, keeping all the smoke in his chest, holding it as long as he could. He handed her the cigarette, she breathed too and gave it back to him.

"You don't want it?" he asked.

"Yeah, I'm awright."

He thought: she was already high, that's why she was so nice. He looked at her, there was something very mellow, rhythmic but slow about her. Yes, she was high. He breathed some more, God, that was a long time, he could feel the taste in his mouth, his whole mouth getting sweet and cool, his body becoming solid, one whole thing, his body being one, and his gestures being cut in a solid mass of air, all is dense, solid, solid. He gets up.

"Let's walk baby."

"Yeah, let's walk."

Good. It was good to communicate like that. No words. It was nice to get along so well. Let's walk: Okay, let's walk. Not a single useless word. Just get up and walk. They were dancing, it was on the very edge of the walk, their bodies swung; the night is goddam sweet. He looked at her, the whole world was switching along with his head as it turned. Lord, it's good to be the world's center, and she was laughing silently, like just having a ball with the walk. Great God almighty, was she having a ball!

"You're stoned, baby," he said.

"Yessuh boss," she swang back. "High as a Georgia pine!"

The world softened. Music. Everything was music, sound, rhythm and bare line of song. He was digging in a thick ocean of rhythm and sheer number. There was a long line of rhythm in his body and he was like wet cotton, mellow and real. The world softened a little more, he felt his muscles relax, his eyes, his ears, the skin all over his body. Calm. Calm. World made slow rhythm, body made loose. Life is a ball. I am a wall; no a bird; no, I am the visible, touchable hearable nobody. He realizes he's kissing the chick in the middle of the street because he feels her tongue in his mouth like a big grotesque cake of flesh. Shit! He thinks, that don't feed! And he feels her body against his. He takes her hand and says:

"Let's go and fuck baby. C'mon!"

Yes, let's go somewhere and drown, drown. . . . He was high, sure he was high. Thick world, and every gesture is a dance. They walked. He was holding her, it was funny how real her body was under his hand. Such a continuity! . . .

"I . . ." He had started a sentence but he'd forgotten what he wanted to say. Things went too fast in that

slow life. Don't talk. Hold it, man, hold it! Yeah . . .
Let it be long wave of life rolling against the sound of
my walk. Not a word.

"Man, that was some nice stuff! . . ."

He smiled. Yeah, that was some beautiful stuff. She
responded to his hand's appeal and there he was, kissing
her again, his eyes wide open; he saw she had a nice-
looking skin, kind of coffee-brown but thin . . . thin and
silky. He was there kissing her and it was good to kiss
that mouth, just good like hot cornbread when you're
hungry.

The street was almost empty now, and silent. It was
probably pretty late. He looked at the houses, the
stores, all that dirt over the street. That was a funky
scene! He laughed.

Let's go get drowned. So deep, Lord, so deep! A man
was passing by. Looking rough. He called him.

"Hey Brer, look-a-here!"

The man stopped.

"What's the matter with you?"

"Look ace, no point gittin mad. I just want to say
hello. . . ."

"Well man, you're fucked up, you'd better take that
bitch home and get some sleep before you git some
trouble!" The man went away. He stood there, like
stunned. The girl was laughing her head off, she
couldn't stop laughing.

"Oh man!" She was trying to put words into her

laughter. "Oh man! That was something else, sayin hello to Chuck!" She kept laughing.

"You know him?"

"Yeah, I know Chuck. Everybody know Chuck here!" She started laughing again.

He went back to walk. She followed, laughing silently, as though sobbing. He was thinking: let's go and get drowned. Let's go smoke again. Let's go fuck. Get so deep. Shit, it's nice that natural world. Everything in its place. Nice. Close to the rush in the blood.

The bar was closed when they got there.

"We'll have to go by the back door," he said. She held his hand tight and he turned around the house. He walked up to his door. The whole house was silent. He put the key in the lock, and gently pushed her in. She put on the light and there they were, sitting on the bed. Get drowned. Lord, back home and so far away from home! Get drowned. They both took their shoes off. She walked to the mirror, got her handkerchief out of her pocket and rubbed off the lipstick. There, he thought. There. He lay down on the bed and she comes along his side. It's so soft. His hand walks over her body, breasts, belly, sex, thighs. . . . Lord, so soft. Loud beat in him, loud music in his head, it's like a whole band he'd hear, from far away. Get drowned. His hand over her belly, her breasts, her sex. He gets up. They both undress. No more light. Her skin against his. So soft, great God, so silky. Lord, it's good to get drowned like that, good to fuck like that. Shit, he should be high all the time, everything in its place, so deep. . . .

She sleeps. He stays there, lying on his back, he can see a little bit of Mississippi summer night through the half-open window. He can smell the night, its taste of dried fried fish, of bad oil, of rotten fruit. . . . A terrible fear and anguish floats in the small room. That world! That killer! Mississippi night, Maurice burnt, his father jailed, his mother dead starving, Gloria jailed, Mary getting high and making love for one dollar, Richie saying that's my life, I gotta take care of it, Richie happy, me hittin that poor motherfucker in Jackson because he said he didn't hate me, and Doudou, oh Doudou whom I look for, because he probably knew the answer. He's slowly getting down, the world is sharpening, he looks at the sleeping body and he wants to jump, fly away. . . . What is my life going to be. Am I gonna sleep my whole life in that room and work in a brickyard in the daytime, or go back to a plantation and pick cotton, or apply for a job as a clerk in some office and die because I won't be able to talk to the white clerks the way I should? Or go back to New York and smile and go to parties and forget about Mississippi nights and cotton-picking and kids sleeping on the ground . . .

Dread. Why us? Dread. Nobody is sure of being alive when tomorrow comes. Anguish made burning. Burning. Get drowned in the fire. Hell. Sleep.

**104**

He wakes up. Mary is there, her soft body lying, motionless on the bed, crawling against his side, her breath caressing his skin. He can feel the warmth of her sleep. A wave of anger and desire rolls over him. He gave a long look at the small lousy room; there was a kind of jubilation that he wanted to find: he was there, safe, free. But no, he didn't feel anything. Then, there was the hot taste of his dead excitement of last night. He'd been real high. He tried to remember when he'd made love to Mary, but it was like dreamy, he knew what, but not how. He kept looking all around the room, he saw the flat hot light through the window, and suddenly became aware of the noises. The whole sound. He listened carefully, trying to figure the time by recognizing the noises. Yeah, they were market noises. It was morning.

Wake up. Wake up man! One more day, whoo, life is scaring when you wake up. Life naked, ugly as a bone. He notices the stick, the one they hadn't smoked, put on the chair. He wonders one minute whether or not he's going to smoke it right now. Early in the morning before he gets really aware, before the fear can settle down in his stomach. Go back to the music and the blindness right away, hardly awakened. He looks at Mary. She'd have to smoke too. They both had some inner fire and violence to throw water on. Smoke on. He took the stick, put it into his pocket. He wasn't going to smoke. He had important things to do, something to look for. He'd get high later. He sank into bed, took Mary's shoulders into his hands, and stuck his body against hers. Have a mercy Lawd, this girl is really sweet! She opens her eyes, smiles and shuts them again. He holds her tight, feeling the thin skin of her belly against his. He doesn't want to think about anything but this flesh, this close and soft flesh. No anguish there, very simple flesh, very beautiful. She wakes up. He felt her hands gripping his back with a kind of despair; she was pulling his neck to her, not wanting to wake up: she too was refusing life. He kissed her gently on the lips, and then in the neck, patting her. . . .

"Baby, baby . . ."

"Ah! Shit. . . ." She got up. Where does her life lead? How can that be a life? Millions of people whose first word early in the morning is Shit! And the little corners of pure life everyone keeps hidden somewhere, deep down, tracked, found, killed, lynched. Shit! . . .

Can a man realize the very dimension of his life? He was thinking, can I? Do I really know what precise amount of horror is involved in mine?

She got up, and looked around the bed. Then she went back to bed. He touched her shoulder.

"Dig Mary . . ."

"What? . . ." She was sleepy. Hangover. He was talking very low, as though he didn't really want to wake her up.

"Can you lend me two dollars?"

"Okay man, but I need 'em. Pay me back when you get 'em. Take them from the wallet, in my pocket. The right one."

She went back to sleep. He walked slowly to the chair, took the wallet out of the dress. There were several one-dollar bills, two fives, one ten, and one twenty. Shit, he thought, she got a whole lotta bread. He took two ones, and shut the wallet. He looked back at her. She was sleeping silently, turned toward the wall, her hands still drawing an empty grip. . . . He opened the wallet again, took out the twenty-dollar bill, folded it several times until it was smaller than a coin and put it in his pocket, while he kept the two ones in his hand. Without a word, he put the wallet back in the red dress. He put the two one-dollar bills in his shirt pocket. He would eat today, and he'd buy some new clothes. He bent over Mary's body and put his lips on her neck, a long kiss. He went down the stairs, walked into the bar. It was empty. He walked out into the street, and the sun slapped his eyes. Ain't nothin like being high, he thought, but the worst is to have been high. He started walking. He looked around, it was probably about eleven thirty, women went marketing; there were kids playing in the middle of the street. My people. It was like going back in the world after a long absence. He'd been away. Too long, he thought, too long!

Once Doudou had walked in the room, and several whites were there. He was drunk. He'd looked at us, looked at the crowd of grays and started shouting.

"Everywhere I go they ask me: you a black American? Fuck that shit! There ain't no black Americans. Americans are white. An American Negro, that don't exist. My grandma she was born in Africa. I am an African."

He stays a minute on the sidewalk, not recognizing the street, not seeing there the same rhythm that blew in it the night before, with Doudou's image swinging before his eyes, something shining back from that very simple past. The sun is high up in the ironhard sky, and it's like he can't walk under that light.

Doudou had been a weird lonely figure in his life. They used to go out together, and Doudou knew everybody in Harlem, or that's what he had thought, for he didn't really know Harlem. Doudou would take him to different places, bars filled up with hustlers and prostitutes, and he'd say:

"Here man, meet Dan. He's a nigger. Mad as hell!"

And he'd laugh. They'd drink and get high and maybe pick up one or two girls. Doudou always did things that scared him a little, like endlessly tearing that sheet hiding the dream's underworld. One day they'd been picked up by the cops and taken to the police station. One of the cops had started cursing because, while being pushed in, Doudou had bumped into the man who held a cup of coffee and the coffee had run over his pants. The cop was real mad. Doudou didn't say a word, he was just laughing all way along, just laughing, and the more he laughed the madder the cop got. Suddenly, Doudou's laughter had broken. He had stood up real stiff, he'd spat upon the floor and looked at the white man straight in the eyes. The cop stopped, like stoned dead. Doudou burst out in laughter and the cop was there, motionless, silent, not daring to understand what had taken place.

He thinks he's going to buy himself a pair of pants and a shirt and maybe new shoes at the pawnshop, and maybe then he'll go and look for a job, but right now he's gonna knock hisself out and eat somethin good and big, 'cause Lawd have a mercy, he's hungry as a motherfucker, like he ain't eaten for days!

The terrifying thing with Doudou is unlike most cats, he didn't think about whites all the time. He even refused to think about 'em. He denied them any right to interfere with his existence. He wanted his whole life to happen in black, and eventually throw the white sonofabitch outta the club. . . . That was frightening enough, because Doudou really did live like that, in a world where there were no whites. And I am sure, he thought many times, I am sure Doudou could have real good white friends. I haven't heard he ever had any, but I'm sure it wouldn't bother him. It was funny how resentless Doudou's violence was. Something like a functional violence against stupidity, like whipping a vicious kid's ass. And calmly he provoked situations where he'd have to whip, and there hadn't ever been a glance of personal hatred in his eyes. Maybe that's what Richie meant, saying I shouldn't let them rob my life, yeah, maybe that's what he meant!

He felt the need to see Richie again, ask him if that's what he'd meant. I'll save a dollar and go back there, he thought.

New York . . . That had been some life! Nights and nights and more nights and them walks with Doudou all through the tremendous life of Harlem. The numbers and all that stuff. And the hep ones down the Village, the ones that wanted to be respectable, and who measured respectability with dollars, and they knew Freud and Kafka and they talked about 'em as though they'd been to school together, and those that loved the Country Blues so much, it is such a pure music, really the soul of American Negro music my dear! . . . Dear my ass! all them sonso'bitches talkin that crap about us being clean and good husbands and moral and profoundly sane in spite of all. Shit! And they forget about them that was born anywhere because there hadn't been any other place where they could be born, and them that went to the chain gang as soon as they could because it was the only place that beautiful American world had reserved for them, and those who wouldn't ever know how to read and who had so many things to forget they hadda drown their memories in wood alcohol or cocain, and the kids who saw their father kicked in the ass by the same clean world twenty times a day and the world used to take the form of any young white trash's foot and wouldn't nobody do nothing because they were a thousand for a hundred and some tried to do something and they died, and many more tried and they died too and folks get so goddam tired of having nothing to do but choose between two kinds of death. . . .

He went to the pawnshop and bought a pair of pants, a shirt and a pair of shoes. He got out and walked back to the bar. Richie was sitting there. When he walked in the fat man got up and the warm smile widened on his face.

"Look-a-here young man! What you know!"

He walked to him and put his hand in the big hand. They sat down. It's a drag, this feeling I have that nothing is for real. He was seeing the bar, Richie, thinking of the girl sleeping upstairs, thinking of a little black belt's whole small life in a little Mississippi country town, and he wondered whether he would ever be able to look at it the way he probably did when he was here twenty years ago, a kid. Maybe didn't nobody feel at home here, maybe the horror was just that everyone felt like not being here to stay, like just spending a few years here, waiting to be lynched, or jailed, or to die of hunger, shame or anger, just waiting for the day it gets too much and kill any white kid, because since death is coming anyway, it might as well be for something real. He remembered the kid he'd been and how that kid had said, when Maurice hadn't been anything but a burnt body swinging and stinking, that he, Dan, would rape and kill a white woman some day, on purpose, with no other reason but evil hatred, because at least there would be one man to be lynched for a good reason.

He took a dollar bill out of his pocket and handed it to Richie.

"Here man, you see, it wan't be so bad an investment!"

Richie laughed.

"Okay, young man, you win."

He ordered a whole meal. That would be over a dollar, but he was really hungry. Richie brought the food and kept sitting there while he started to eat. He thought: it's weird, it's like there is something very tight between him and me. Something like a silent complicity.

"The chick, still up there?"

The big warm roar sounded again.

"No man, she went down and split. She said for you to see her tonight where she was last night."

"That all she said?"

"Yeah. She's cute man, real cute babe. I know her, she work down the street. She's a tough babe. Straight. Don't bother nobody, mind her own business. . . . Of course some people just don't like that kind o' gal, but no sweat, huh?"

"Right man, right. Like you say, that's one's own life, ain't it?"

"There you go young fella, talkin my language!"

They laughed, and he kept eating silently. Lord, was he hungry! The food melted in his mouth like butter, one second he thought: if this could never end!

He sees in his memory the cabin where he was born, and the earthy ground where he slept when the small house crowded. They used to call it: the farm, it gave them a feeling of importance, a farm, and they forgot about how little the house was, how desperately bare. Sometimes his mother would cook some tapioca and the middle of the tapioca was like butter in his mouth. . . . Soft, Lord, so soft! He was sure he'd never forget the taste of the tapioca in his mouth.

No, that's not what he meant, I'm sure it's not what he meant, saying I shouldn't let them steal away my life. I'm sure he didn't mean to fight without hatred. He don't know what fight is. He's a bald-headed Uncle Tom tryin'a pretend he's having a ball in that crap. I should ask him. But how? There was a kind of barrier of warmth and good humor protecting the man's real identity. He felt it as something almost physical, like a plastic folder or a nylon bag behind which the real man would live and feel, all that within that tiny protected space, and nothing can get out of the bag.

There must be something wrong with that man. He's just too cool. And suddenly he understood. It was funny how clearly he saw it. Why ask, he thought, why shake it? Sadistic motherfucker, that's what I am! He was still eating, Richie was looking at him with a kind of patient satisfaction, there was no expression on his face, just a great warmth, and he was seeing Richie with the corner of his glance. Why shake it? That man had built himself a little quiet world of peace and love and defeat in the midst of a nightmare, and who would think he hadda break that world, break that peace and love? Who, why, to get him where? Who would decide that this man's life had to be bloody for real because his quietness was a living lie and nightmare? What the hell am I worrying about that cat for? Thousands and thousands of kids down here are virtually murdered every day because they can't accept, because they are not capable of building up that goddam living lie of a life! He was still watching Richie while eating, pretending he didn't mind anything but his plate. Shit! he slowly whispered in his spoon. Where the hell am I gonna find a man? He finished his glass, gave Richie another dollar bill, and a little change, got up and walked upstairs to his room. He sat down on the bed, there was a record being played somewhere in the house. Some Blues. He started undressing and put the old clothes on the bed. He walked to the mirror, half-naked and looked at the dim image of his dark-brown body. He was tired. So tired. Lord . . . He advanced his face until it was almost against the mirror and plunged his glance into his own eyes. There was nothing to see, nothing to discover. Just a tired-looking brown face with a beard. Nothing to see. He stood there a while, naked in the middle of the small lousy room, awkward body not knowing what to do with itself. After a while, he walked back to the bed, like regretfully, and put on the new clothes.

He had seen Gloria again. Last year. He had wanted to keep her with him, but she had gone again, and a few weeks later he had learnt she had been caught while stealing and she was in jail. It had been like the breaking of a very subtle string in his chest. Like being sure of Gloria's death for him.

This goddam life just don't advance. He's lying on the bed again, things keep happening the way they used to. Ain't nothing changing, ever. It's a drag.

It had been a terrible crack in his life. For Gloria was the only link he'd kept with a simple part of his past. A very shining world, that had to do with his being a child maybe, but also there was an actual purity. It's funny, he thinks, how my life switched from the very pride and innocence of those days to this tired body obscenely standing up in a room. Almost closed circle. Forty miles. Yes, there was pride and health, and some kind of bloody dignity. Closed circle. Maybe

**116**

Doudou is what Maurice would have become if he had lived. Maybe that's one same soul to find back. There were hundreds of faces crowding the small hotel room now. Have a mercy, he said, aloud, and his voice was deep and clean all of a sudden. There was a kind of bloody dignity. . . . What's changed? What to hell has rotted in ourselves? Closed circle. We'll be dry again, some day, oh yes! Nothing is dead, that fire is just being born again. . . . I gotta do something about my life, he says slowly, before anybody can mess it up. Yeah, I gotta do something. He lies down on the bed, the room is very small. He lies down. Do something. Life is simple.

Look for that violence! . . . Where? Maurice had died. His father had died one day. Died of anger. It had been very simple the way he'd died, stiff and proud because he'd rather die than accept to leave town. He'd gotten up one Sunday morning in church, and the preacher was his own brother. He'd walked up to the pulpit and cursed his brother out, saying he was tired of listening to the same old lies all the time, about the last ones being the first ones, and love the white murderer of your children; and the whole congregation was like stunned, staring in horror and amazement at that man, my father, whom they had known for years, and who was calm and honest and polite with everybody; who did his work conscientiously; that man red with anger and holding his own brother by the collar, throwing him down to the ground and shouting to the people in the church to go home, there would be no sermon today; and he was a short worthy man, very poor and very proud. . . .

He gets up. The straight figure of his father dances before his eyes like the light of a candle. He thinks of the twenty dollars he has taken out of Mary's wallet and he wonders why he can't feel guilty. . . . His father would have whipped him to death if he had stolen a penny, when he was a kid. And he never did. But now, it had no reality, he couldn't even imagine what it meant to steal twenty dollars. He needed them, he wanted them and he'd taken 'em. Period. He tried to find a little guilt in himself, but no, nothing. He had gotten over guilt: he had felt too much for no reason, it didn't mean a thing to him any longer. Still, he thought, it's BAD! But it was ridiculous, what's BAD? What does it mean? Maybe nothing was bad or good for him, maybe that was part of being a Negro in America in the twentieth century. . . . What would Mary say when she'd find out about the twenty bucks? She'd be mad. Sure she'd be mad allright, but then? Yeah, maybe it's bad because she'll be mad, and it'll be my fault. He was trying to reason sharply, but he couldn't, all that had no reality, maybe Mary had stolen the money herself, and so what, what else could she do, he thought, ain't nobody but thieves what can make a little money come into the black belt, I wonder how people would make out without 'em!

After that, the Klan had sent letters to his father, saying he hadda leave town within a week, otherwise they'd kill him. He'd taken the letters to the sheriff and said: look, you're honest, what these people do is illegal, you got to prosecute them. The sheriff had put him in jail, saying he was himself a member of the Klan, and he'd keep him in jail eight days, and then let him go, so the Klansmen would lynch him because he hadn't left town. My father was still red with anger, and the next morning, when the sheriff had opened the jail to see him, he'd found the little stiff man dead, with a red mask of anger over his black skin.

There is something in him like a long sigh, wanting to fly away. That life sticks to the dirty ground. Can't there be a minute of freedom in the gestures, in the way I can look at the sky? Life sticking to the dust, every day a little narrower, a little more tightly linked to the agony of the worm that twists its bloody rings on the sand. He remembers Europe; waking up in the morning in Brittany, with nothing to eat and no money, and he was happy, yes he was really happy because there was the sea and that fresh sky and he'd walk everywhere he'd want. . . . Bullshit he says aloud, bullshit! What if they took you for an Arab in Paris, what did you read in their eyes in the subway? How much denial? He is laughing, because really, such a fucked up world it's unbelievable, it goes far beyond the most monstrous imagination. . . .

Gloria hadn't been surprised to see him again. I'd always been sure, she'd said, that we'd see each other again. They had talked quietly of the things past, the many things that had passed, and the people who had died, and those who had been forgotten, buried deep down in the memory's filth. It was some bright bit of their lives breathing again for a while, their lives that had been, hers as well as his, a long drag of misery, wondering and violence; it was weird, they were for each other the very symbol of that clean life that had gone, that proud and honest life, that motionless dignity of Maurice's body, all their hopes of wisdom and all their love, all that which had died under the tumbling walls of their brain, buried under the spittle, the wounds, the insults, the cold, and hunger and anger and hatred and cruelty. . . . He put the shoes on and opened the door. I hope Richie is not downstairs. I don't feel like talkin to him. He walks down the stairs, slowly, thinking of Doudou again, starting to hear a deep rumor in his mind that was born a long time ago but which he only starts listening to. We ain't all Richies and Dans and Uncle Toms and crazy killers.

There are more people like my father. There are thousands of Doudous ready to be born and to fight for love and dignity. There must be millions. He got to the bar and walked to Richie. The fat man looked at the pants and the shirt, and the shoes, and smiled.

"Hmmm Hmmm! Look at that, my! Ain't you somethin, good-lookin like you goin'a git married right now an' your little ol' bride she waitin for you! . . . Where you goin, dressed up sharp like that and all?"

"Out Richie. I'm goin out. I found an answer."

"An answer to what?"

"To something that involves you and me and many more people, brother, an answer to a question that was asked long ago, like you said, a too long time ago!"

"Ace, ace," said Richie, "take it easy, take care where you goin, don't go too far, don't go too fast. . . ."

"Don't worry about me, big brer, I know my way around, I ain't gonna fall down on my way. Here, take the key, I'll be back tonight, but I don't know when. If you see Mary, you just tell her what I said, and that she don't worry. . . ."

Richie stayed there, up in the middle of the room, like stunned by his new rapidity and determination. He walked out fast. He had something to do. A kind of pilgrimage. But it would be a test too. He put his hand in his pocket and pulled out some money. He counted. There were seven dollars and a few cents left. Allright he said. A few people passed by him and there was

121

probably something funny about him because they gave him amazed looks. Then he realized. It's because he walked fast, real fast and stiff just like a white man. . . . He laughed. He started to walk a little more slowly, and putting that loud rhythmic beat in his walk. There, he said, There. Come back, brer, come back, this is the land of the dream, come back, and he looked in the street, stared at the faces, men, women, girls and all of them, everyone of them had an intimate knowledge of death and violence, everyone of 'em slept every night with fear and they all had the same bullet of warm cotton in their stomachs which he called anguish. He looked at them and there was a hot tenderness in his glance. That's why we are so close to each other, that's why! All the same familiar monster in the belly, we recognize it when we meet, and we call each other brothers and sisters because after all, since we share the same interiors, we might as well forget about distances. He walks. Yeah, his life is a closed circle. But he gotta close it now, there is one more step to do, he gotta lock it up and remain out of it so it'll be all past and dead, all past and dead nightmare.

# IV

I'll go back to Clarksdale, he thought. I'll go back there and see. Just see the farm, the path where I met Gloria, see the town, the square where they'd taken Maurice and the hill where they hung and burnt him. There was a cold resolution in his mind. I'll go back there. Anyway, I won't ever succeed, I won't ever achieve this total awareness I keep lookin for. Impossible. It's too big, as soon as I become conscious of something new I forget a part of what I knew. I'll just go back there because anger will thus be fixed in my mind for a good while. And I know that might not be the worst, but I need it as a sign, something to cling to. And I know Doudou lives in me, in everyone of us, the point is just to let him grow, to give him space. He was going to close that circle for good. And maybe a new man would grow up, spring from the earth, maybe somebody who would be really free, free of hatred, a new man who would fight with fervor and no personal passion. . . . He wondered whether that was possible. He was walking toward the bus stop, thinking of the millions of brothers and sisters who lived in the middle of a bloody puddle of dream and threat and who still hadn't resigned, still raised their kids, trying to make men and women out of them. . . . Has my will disappeared? Has my anger vanished, my hatred died? Yeah, maybe all that had gone away, had been blown away by something bigger, a greater anger and will, of a different kind. Maybe that was the beginning of the new circle. Maybe he'd find out a way for all those who had to hate and smile to take the dark glasses off once for all. He smiled, thinking there was a created race somewhere in the world, a race of several million people who all wore sunglasses day and night because it was cheaper than gin or heroin and it protected almost as well.

He got to the bus stop. He would have to wait two hours. He was nervous about the bus; there were always incidents in buses, because colored people were supposed to sit in the back and there was always a cracker looking for trouble who would try to start a fight or something like that. He hated the idea of having to sit there with that tension paralyzing him, and that faked carelessness with which all the Negroes sitting there would talk to each other, softly, and everyone pretending their being in the back was casual, as though they didn't even know why. . . . I'll walk on the road, and maybe a car will take me. He didn't want to admit that he wanted to walk on the road because he was getting scared of his involvement with people, Richie, Mary, and he wanted to find back that freedom he'd felt on the road. But maybe he didn't even know himself that was the reason.

He walks. How come my whole life is taking the form of a walk? For days and days he ain't been doing nothing but walking. Stop somewhere man! He was talking alone, and some people looked at him with compassion and sorrow. He noticed it. They too think I'm cracked up. Stop somewhere man. Stop! I gotta walk forty more miles before I can stop. I gotta close the circle of my past life for good. Make sure it won't open again. Maybe I'm getting old. Maybe one has to get old and know that doubt, maybe one must go through that weakness of the man who is not sure of anything. He was hearing his own voice, like out of a longgone dream: look for that sure violence, look for it day and night! He sighed. He'd have to go back to that search, because there was nothing else to do, because he knew that violence was the only healthy track for him. But that would be later, right now he had a very important part of his life to visit and pen up.

**127**

He was out of town now. Just where he'd stopped. He remembers: I'm black and it's good. He laughed. I really don't know how good it is. I swear the Lord I know it's not wrong, I know it should be good, but right now . . . That's a whole lotta crap, he thinks, to hell with them words, what I'm gonna say or think ain't gonna change nothin of what actually is! But he knew the words were also part of the dream.

Days and nights in Europe he hadn't thought of anything but having a ball. Just go out in the evening, go and dance, get high and listen to some music. He'd heard some real good music in Europe. One night he'd had a fight with a white G.I. from Chicago, a northern cracker, and he'd cut the man's face. He'd left the cat bleeding on the sidewalk, holding his cut face with his hands and silently crying, really crying, but no sound could get out of his throat, it was as if he'd had his voice cut too. He'd gotten back in his hotel room that night, and something had burst out in him, like suddenly becoming aware of all that blood, of that useless violence. He was seeing the man's image, with the blood running over his fingers, like trying to hold it back, and he'd tried to remember why the fight had started; as the night passed, he was still awake and he had gotten real sure there had been no reason, definitely no reason but some inner rage wanting to come out. Why not he thinks, they're responsible for that violence thrown back upon them, they created it, fed it with their own violence and hatred. . . . But he knew there had been something wrong in the way he'd cut the cat's face. Not that he shouldn't have done it, but there had been a minute when he'd lost control, when he'd been totally involved in a kind of sadistic rage and pleasure. God, he sighed, is this what they've made of us?

To know nothing. Not to be sure of anything but of that helpless rage. Just that something goes wrong there, that something is rotten in that life. Just know it's an impossible world to live in, but have to survive. How can a man live upon such assumptions, he wondered, how can I?

A car was coming near. Looking back he could see the driver, a young white man, and there was another fellow with him, young too. He got nervous. They were the kind that want to show how superior they are, that want to ascertain their power all the time. He didn't know them, but he knew that right away. It's terrible, he thought, how people's feelings get obvious on their faces. The car almost stopped about a hundred feet behind him. He didn't look back again, for he knew they were waiting for him to do anything so they could have a reason to beat him. He walked toward the ditch, wanting to be as far from the place where the car would pass as he could. The car behind him also started to run along the ditch, very slowly, so as to keep the same distance between them. He slowed, the car slowed. He was real afraid. What are these motherfuckers goin to invent? He'd thought aloud, and he was almost frightened by the sound of his own voice, for there was something like a murderous coldness in it. He was still walking with a sophisticated softness and calm, as though he hadn't even seen the car. Suddenly he heard the noise of the engine running like mad; he hardly had the time to jump on his right and plunge into the ditch. The car passed by, terribly fast, the car's right door wide open, like sweeping the road's side, and he felt the violent wind projected ahead. They had thought he wouldn't have time to avoid the door. The shock would probably have killed him. He heard the voice of the younger one, who had blocked the open door with a long iron stick, howling.

"Get out the way, nigger!"

He stayed a moment lying in the ditch, like stunned. He was not really amazed, he was not surprised, he had known something like that would happen; he was not afraid. His heart was beating like mad, but it's just the excitation of the jump, he thought. He was very cold, looking at the car smallening over there, far away, and thinking of the two blond-headed kids, imagining them laughing at his grotesque jump, knowing they would have forgotten the incident within a couple of hours. He was very cold, it frightened him how cold he was. He realized tears were rolling along his cheeks, frozen tears along his cheeks, but he was not crying. Maybe he was not even mad. He stood there, after he'd gotten up, with the frozen tears rolling along his cheeks; his lips were pressed and closed, there was a kind of cold blindness in his eyes. He started to walk like an automatom, he had in his mind the bright image of two blond-headed kids laughing at the good joke his death would have been. There were no more questions in his mind, no more hesitation. That sure violence, he thought suddenly, that sure violence! He'd found it back. He was walking, stiffening and he didn't even feel the heat of the sun. Walk. The cold was increasing in his chest, there was no warmth, no wonder in him. They will have to disappear, he said. They will have to. They will have to clear out the room for a new man. There was no hatred in his head. It was all very simple, very clean. There was a great anger, but he was not angry at the two kids. They would have to die, they will have to. It was terribly clear in him now. Sickness that had gone out of him into the two condemned kids who would have to die soon because there was a certain amount of death that was involved in the cure. He felt very clean all of a sudden, like washed away, he felt his cold body in all its density. Solid. Now I can go. Now I can go away, the circle is closed, I don't even have to go that far.

Another car was coming. I won't move he thought. Whatever happens I won't move, ain't nobody goin'a laugh this time. He walked, his whole body was tight;

the car is coming near and he walks, stiffer as the seconds pass, I am conscious, he says with a terrible jubilation, I am conscious! The car slowed at his side. There was nobody in the car but a young colored guy with a chauffeur cap. He bit his lips. Ain't that a bitch, he thinks, ain't that a bitch? The cat opened the door and said:

"You're crazy to walk like that, get in!"

He got in the car without a word, the block of cold was still heavy in his stomach. The driver shut the door and the car started.

"Where are you going like that?" He spoke a very pure English.

"Clarksdale."

"Good Lord! Did you think you'd walk forty miles?"

"No. . . . Anyway, I wasn't goin to Clarksdale." He was silent a minute. "This your boss' car?"

"No!" the man smiles. He might be twenty-five. "No, it's my car, but I wear the cap, it helps avoid trouble! . . . But now tell me, what were you doing on that road, trying to get killed or what?"

I won't tell him what happened, he thought. It's no point. He's too young a little brother. What he knows is already too much. What happened belongs to me. I have to safeguard that hateless anger and will. It's mine; I have a duty to fill toward all my little brothers who already know too much of that cold horror.

"Yeah, maybe." He laughed, as though it was a joke.

"No, I was in a hurry and there was no bus, I thought I'd find a car on the road."

The young man smiled. He looked at the countryside behind the window, seeing that road he knew so well pass away, fast, as though it were not the same road. They passed by the fields, and he looked at the left, over the driver's shoulder, trying to see Pearl's cabin in the bottom, Pearl's lost cabin in the canes.

"Do you work here?" It was the polite young man who had spoken. He thought: my clothes must stink of the pawnshop, it's better like that.

"No, I don't work at all."

"Jobs are rather rare, aren't they?"

"I don't know, I didn't look for one, actually. . . ." He looks at the road running under the car, the cold is still in him, that stiff cube of angry ice, and he wonders: why is this man so cold, why can't he just call me brother and slap me on my back and laugh like we do, for no reason, just because laughter is the only friend we can trust . . . Why is there such a distance between us, just because he thinks I can't speak English as well as he does and he's read more than me and he's got that car he can't use as his because crackers don't give a damn how many books niggers read . . . Shucks! Why do these kids get so uppity with us instead of gettin mad at 'em? He looked at the guy's clean hands, clean-cut fingernails and their elegant movement to hold the wheel. Yeah! Grandson of a slave, riding that beautiful car, and his wearing a chauffeur cap is just a slight joke, ain't it? Grandson of a slave and wearing that splendid gold watch, ain't that proof of democracy? Polite, well-educated and all, and so really human and nice, he even stops to save one of his less fortunate brothers, a poorly dressed man walking along the road, a sharecropper probably: and see how marvelous this young man is, he talks to the worker, yeah, because he hasn't forgotten his grandfather wan't but a slave! . . .

"I reckon you's a student or some . . ."

"Yes, I live in Tuskegee, but I'm now on vacation at my girl friend's. She lives here in Mississippi. Clarksdale. Her parents live with her but they are traveling up North for the moment. So, she is alone."

He didn't say a word. He was trying to remember Doudou's face and it was funny, he couldn't see it clearly, it always took him back to Maurice's soft smile and enormous laughter. Maybe they're all one same man he thought, Maurice and Doudou and my father and all those who work and sweat for a little more dignity. He was seeing, like in a flash, the opened door of a car and two blond-headed kids running toward the inevitability of death. People are thick. They're irreducible. There is a part of their reality that stubbornly remains one, that can't be split. The young man was still smiling. Maybe he thinks life is beautiful; no, these kids are the sickest of us all, cause

134

they don't even know why they suffer any longer. He looked at him and extended his hand.

"My name is Daniel Peebles."

"And mine is Ken. Kenneth Dukes. Hello!"

"Hello!"

Don't that cat realize he's ridiculous? He was trying to hold back his laughter: hello! Could you figure that out? Hello! This fellow is nuts: hello! He was silent again. My solid and cold anger, I gotta safeguard you, I gotta protect you, for we have so much to do, so much work, he looked at the young man driving, so much to undo, so much to rectify, go back deep down in our stolen childhoods and find back that fraternity. . . .

"And you," Ken asked, "what do you do?"

"I'm a tourist," he said, very seriously. The man laughed.

"Are you?"

"Yeah, sure, isn't it obvious?"

He thought: now he's wondering what sort of a funny sharecropper I am. Ken was looking at him with a kind of distrustful curiosity.

"Aren't you from here?"

"Yessuh, I was born right here allright. . . . But I been away, a long, long time! And after a few years, I said to myself, Dan, you gotta go and check up what happenin in that good ol' Miss, and I answered to myself, why not, why wouldn't I practice tourism in my own country, it's the least I can do, ain't it?"

Ken did not know whether he should laugh or not. Was he kidding?

"Is that how it happened?"

"Jus' like I tole you. And now here I am, ridin that nice-lookin car of yours and folks will even think you're my driver and I am some African minister touring incognito through that dear old Southland, just to make sure that all them lies about segregation and all that crap is built up by communist propaganda and sick white-haters. Man! I'm tellin you, ain't just nothin like tourism!"

"You're funny. . . ." He could see how embarrassed Ken was. "You sound very bitter. . . ."

"I'm funny? Man! Who's funny, you find it strange that a man is bitter, here, and I'm the one what's funny? Did you ever really look around yourself? When you leave your college in your big beautiful car, don't you ever think of takin a walk in the fields and see how your people live? Listen, don't you think in spite of your car and your watch you're far more bitter than me?"

"I don't understand you. . . ."

"Don't mess with it man, don't try to understand, it'd cost you too much to even try. But let me ask you one question: Do you think you got so much to lose?"

"But . . . We're making progress, there have been some changes. . . ."

"Fuck that shit man!" He was shouting now. There was a blond image of two kids in a car before his eyes.

Progress! Fuck that shit man! This what they tell you in your college? That crap's used up man! Progress, changes? Boy! Don't you know better'n that? You think them changes make you more of a man? Don't you think some bigger thing should happen? He kept silent. He was looking at the road, his lips closed, and there was that sure and cold violence in him.

They didn't talk for a while. He was still staring at the road, trying to link this ride with his walk, but it was impossible, it was like two different planets. Maybe the people who have a car don't see the world. Maybe they don't even live in the same world. . . . Ken was driving nervously. After a few minutes, he got his head up, and looked at him, while still watching the road.

"Listen Dan . . ."

Something warm moved in him. Shit, it was good, somebody calling you by your name, somebody talking to you as to a man. He stiffened. He felt the ice cube in his chest getting softer. I must not, he said in his mind. I must not. This anger is the only sane thing I know here. Ain't nobody goin'a wreck it up.

"Listen Dan . . . Excuse me, I don't know why you take it like that, I mean, our relationship . . . I think I know what you feel. . . ."

Lord, how tired he was! Such a long way behind him, and he hadda go deeper, closer to where he'd

**137**

started from. Go back, find back the sure will of those who had never gotten up in a car like this one.

"No Ken, no, you don't know nothing, but you'd like to understand. . . . And the more you go the more you'll find out that all the books you read didn't mean a shit, because they were part of a world where we have no room, where we just simply don't exist. No man! You don't know nothing, and especially not how I feel. And you talk of the only thing you know, progress, changes. . . . Do you also think that we got to be patient, that we got to deserve freedom?"

"Well . . ."

"Man, I'm asking you. Do you think we gotta deserve freedom?"

"I think we should ask for more educational opportunities, because it is the key . . ."

"No man! There ain't no key. . . . There can't be no key. . . . Do you think crackers deserve their freedom and their power, and their murderous arrogance, and their right to kill, to burn, to threaten, to commit genocide? . . . Do you think anyone has to wait, has to fill up conditions to be free? If you'd talked about changes, about progress, to the man who picks cotton, to the man who puts the gas in your big car, to the woman who washes floors, what do you think they'd have said? Don't you know they'd have thought you're kiddin? To whom, for whom these changes? For you, to allow you to be every day a little farther, a little more ignorant every day about how your own people live and die? But what for them? What can change for them, except everything? Listen Kenneth, every day you and me think a little more that we are Negroes and it means something peculiar, that it means a way of lookin at the world that ain't nobody else got. And at the same time, that we gotta hide it, and claim we're all alike, all men brothers on the face of the earth, and extend our hands to all forgetful killers. . . . And I say, allright, but the truth is that our fuckin racism fucks up the whole scene, because the point ain't, the point never was whether or not we're different. For a man is born to be free, whatever he is. For whether we're Negroes or we were made Negroes by their immense sickness is not the point. Listen to me, Ken, we don't have no point to make of our ability to be free. We don't have no proof to furnish of our intelligence, of our honesty, of our courage. . . . We don't have nothing to do but fight to death for a stolen freedom that's ours. What do you think proofs are going to give? Do you think whites enslaved several million men and women because those men and women were supposed to be inferior? Don't you know all that shit came later? Do you think the sharecropper I once was felt better off because some scholar had found out the ancient Egyptians were black? Do you think he felt more related to Ramses II because of that? Man! I tell you, let's not make the problem a question of genetics.

Fuck all that crap! Three hundred years ago our ancestors were brought here from Africa to work as slaves on plantations. Who are you going to convince when you write a book and say that the people brought here were civilized? Don't we know it already? Haven't we always known how much humanity was in our souls, and how three hundred years of whitening helplessly tried to wash away that love and that dignity? Can't you see it down in yourself, don't you know you're a man? Oh boy! Did they make you forget you're a man and do you have to write a book they won't read to make it sure for yourself? Do you think them crackers down here that don't want to see a boot in a car and that make you wear a chauffeur cap are responsible for Shakespeare's genius? Man! Life is terribly simple you know, for we don't know anything about it. Because we keep looking at the surface of things and we're afraid of seeing how far from our lousy words life really takes place. Don't nobody deserve freedom man! If I could talk to a white man and just tell him what's in my heart this's what I would say: Give it back, fuckin thief, give it back! You talk about an education we gotta ask for: no man, THEY have to repair a moral and physical damage done to twenty million souls, including yours and mine, because there was no other reason to their crimes but greed and sickness and piracy and profit and gratuitous cruelty. . . . And we don't have to be humble. We don't have to be patient. For three hundred years we have succeeded in living within an underworld of fear and degradation, and we have succeeded in keeping, you and me excepting, a fantastic vitality and strength, because we have learnt out of slavery more than any other men, and because we know more about life and men than anybody else . . . but fuck that racism man! We're man and we gotta right to have all that men can have. You just can't say suffering is more natural to us, because you couldn't suffer a tenth of what my father went through and you're blacker than him, and he never said a word until two days before he died and he didn't think he should go to college in order to have a right to be free, and he was angry because he knew men were men and he didn't give a fuck about what color Mozart was because what he wanted was a decent life and Mozart died too long ago to give anybody a house or a good job. And his last message was to fight to death because really it just can't last no longer and this here world is becoming a big sack of shit and we have kids to raise. . . ."

His voice broke. . . . What was the point? Could Ken understand this? Shit, ain't he black just like me? But he knew it was not true. Ken was desperately looking for something he'd never find: a place in that same rotten racist world. And he didn't care about a better place for everybody in a world that would have changed, for he loved this one, for he was part of this world and incapable of conceiving another one. Poor kid! he thought. There will be no peace for him. Waking up and hating his own goddam face in the mirror, waking up in the morning and wondering why to hell was HE born black, and there ain't goin'a be no peace for him. . . .

Ken was still driving silently, his eyes stuck to the road. He wondered whether he shouldn't have just shut up and let this young man drive his way, drive his life with his elegant hands all through this bloody country. What good is it goin'a do? He was slightly ashamed of his need to hurt the young man. Shucks, he knows that as well as me, why did I have to recall it? Cold and warm. Ice and love. How can that be? He watched Ken's nervous eyes, and he knew there was a very slight string still linking them to each other, and it had been very close to being broken. Deep down, something like a thin tenderness . . . He slowly caressed his lips with his fingers. Maybe it's because he's black. . . . Because he's still got some of that anguish in him, maybe even more. . . .

"Maybe you're right." Ken's voice was slow, he could feel how difficult it had been for the young man to talk, to say this. "Maybe you're right. But I don't know. . . ."

He didn't answer. He'd hurt him. He'd hurt him allright. Why? There was a far voice in his mind, talking. Why? Lord! He mentally tried to justify. Could I know he'd be hurt? How could I know he'd react like that? Most of these kids wouldda said I'm crazy,

142

I'm a Communist, I'm sick white-hater, they wouldda said it's all because our people are lazy and dirty and primitive and all that shit! How to hell could I know this one was sincere?

"You know . . . Dan . . . I think of it sometimes. I know it's true. But you know, we get caught up in such a closed up world, if I said anything like that to my family, they'd think I have become crazy. . . . Like my girl friend, you know, she wouldn't understand this, because she thinks it's all a matter of individuals, that if you really work you can succeed and prejudice will disappear little by little if everybody helps to forget it and we're clean and honest and educated. . . ."

He repressed a kind of bitter laugh. She is just so much convinced of it that's all she can talk about with the boy she loves. Just so obvious she can't think of nothin else. He let his glance go over Ken's dark face. They're so sick! Black, and they don't even know what it means. . . .

"Listen Ken . . ." This's the last thing I'll say he thought, "Listen Ken, you know there are thousands and thousands of kids your age who know that and who are ready to fight and fight and fight. . . . Millions of kids who don't need but a little more self-reliance to shout that truth they know that men are men and anybody who doesn't admit it is a sonofabitch and that they don't have to become white to be accepted and that they don't want to become sick but just be accepted the way they are, and if somebody gotta change it won't be only them because there are thousands and thousands and millions white people in this country that are much farther from humanity than any of us ever was. And you know how much science and love and humanity there is in those ghettos you've never wanted to see? How much we know and you want us to forget, because you think our salvation lies in being as fucked up as the white man? You know that, Ken, millions of kids who don't want to be humble, ever, because we don't have to accept such a bargain, and they stand up man! They stand up and they just don't accept being involved in that sick business of hatred and patience, of deep hatred preaching love, maybe won't even accept that people like you or me claim we gotta right to talk for them. Ain't nobody but themselves goin to talk for them. Oh boy, that might just sound mighty crazy and foolish and dreamlike, but put it in your head and think of it. Don't underestimate your own people man! don't, cause you'd be surprised!"

There was a new silence. After a while Ken asked: "If you don't have anything else to do, would you like to spend the evening with us?"

He imagined his girl friend, the clean house, there'd be drinks and food and records.

"No thank you. Really, thank you, but I want to go back to town before tonight." There was the image of

a car, door wide-opened, sweeping the road's side. . . .
"No thank you," he said again, "anyway, I'm a pretty
bad guest you know. . . . You don't lose too much."

He stopped the car.

"I'll drive you back, then!"

What does he think, he's doing a good action, or
what? Lord! So fuckin much to rectify!

"Thank you, but you don't have to, you know. If
you're in a rush, just drop me somewhere and I'll catch
a bus."

"No, no, I'll drive you back."

He smiled. Okay, if that's what you want.

"Okay, thank you."


They drove back, silently. I want to see Mary, he
thought. I gotta see her. It was strange that need of
her. He remembered her warm body in the morning,
and how she had smiled when she'd first awakened.
Mary is nice, he thinks. Real nice.


Ken was driving very fast. There is something like
a mean little animal in his head that eats him up, he
thinks. A little more and his whole head will have been
eaten. He looks at Ken and there is a bitter irony in his
look. What the hell are we gonna do with you, nigger,
when your whole head's eaten up?

He was driving back silently. There was more softness in the elegant gestures of his hands. Don't worry

boy! You'll have forgotten all this tonight! How could you not? How could you not forget, with your father and your mother and your girl friend who thinks all that doesn't exist and your car. . . . How could you not forget a short conversation with a stinking junky while you've got all these years of college where the white man taught you all the marvels of his world and you're so goddam sure there ain't no other world that's worth being lived, and you're goddam right. How could you not forget, little Ken who wonders why all these prejudiced white people keep saying all colored folks got rhythm while you ain't got it? And you wonder whether it wouldn't be better if we'd just simply had no rhythm, none of us, to prove them wrong. Don't worry, little lost brother, don't worry about that, when you go back to college, they'll tell you, they'll explain it to you, how crazy I am, how crazy you are to even listen to me. . . . They'll give you figures and statistics and laws and tell you you gotta be realistic, and maybe they'll even talk about the safeguard of Western values, of individual property, who knows? No, you just go back to your girl friend and drown your head in her skirts, she'll tell you you shouldn't ever talk with sharecroppers, 'cause they ain't your kind, and why would you resist, it's so nice to be superior, especially when you're among so-called inferiors, and after all, hasn't that beautiful civilization taught you that men were individuals before all, and that the very point of life was success? Go man! Go. . . . You're black and I am black and there is so much we have in common just because of that ridiculous similarity. . . . But go, the very point of life is success they have said, don't give a damn about your neighbor, just wish him good luck, and don't ever try to find out how many seats there are in that big movie house, cause it'd give you blues, ace, the blues, to see how few can get in.

They were getting back in town. They hadn't said a word. The silence had gotten thick, solid. I'm sure he'll be so glad when I'm gone. So glad to be able to start forgetting.

"Where do you want me to drop you?"

They were in front of the bus stop, it wouldn't be but five minutes walking to Richie's.

"Right here."

Ken looked at him, stopped the car.

"Good-bye Daniel. Good luck. I hope to see you again. Sincerely. Good-bye man, thank you."

He laughed.

"Take care of yourself, Kenny, good care."

He slapped the door, started to walk. He knew Ken was still looking at him, he fought against himself not to turn back, he didn't. After a couple of minutes, he heard the car going.

It's like a long fall of old skins, everything rotten and empty, so dry and flat. . . . Long ago, too long ago, there had been something, Richie had said. He had looked for the very minute down in his days past, and he had not been able to find out the time, the place. Something to undo. Maybe it was Man himself, something he had done to his own mind, some kind of mutilation. Original sin; somebody else's sin to pay for; the white man's guilt, and we gotta carry it too . . . No. That's not it either. Our complicity with his guilt and fear, because we had kept a foolish love for wisdom and knowledge, and we had replaced hatred by resentment, murder by hatred. Yes, there was that burial of murder and violence to undo, some kind of uncool surgery to go through. . . . A long time ago. One day, he had thought: I am nobody; and it meant: I would have to change, to go through an actual inner revolution to find my real identity, that manhood that's mine, that's always been mine, but which I don't know. It's a wild scheme, have to go back to the very essence of what I am and find there a new self; something at the same time unknown and very familiar. What are we going to do? Are we going to keep crying it's all their fault and expect their irresponsibility and sickness to repair what they have done? Or can we decide they won't have that chance? That we are ready to assume the whole of mankind's weight; that they haven't killed enough in us, and they're more castrated than us, and they depend on us more than we do on 'em, and that we are capable of no retaliation, because the point is to set everything right, not to enjoy the feeling of the knife moving in the wound. That if we have to kill, we won't have to hate any longer.

Fuckin tricky world. Every word, every step a track. And never leads nowhere but to holes. Traps. Who wins the most in that dubious game? Both Ken and me want that bullshit to end up; but we have different methods, for we don't talk about the same bullshit; and we both prove crackers right as much as wrong, because there are also several kinds of crackers, that don't all get along. Even Doudou was proving them

**149**

right. And Maurice and my father and Gloria and Ken's girl friend, for anyway they ain't ever seeing but half of the truth, not always the same half, and we shouldn't even try to convince'em; not mess with that absurd business of demonstration. Mind our own business, like we'd wake up one day and say: the point ain't what they say, the point must not be what they say or think. The point must be us. What we do, what we say, what we think. But what we do above all.

I am a pretentious motherfucker. I can't do that. Just confuse my own sickness, my own destiny with my people's. Shucks! Everybody does that, ain't nothin wrong with it, we ain't found no other way of living yet.

*Lemme tell you people, lemme talk that talk. It's a tale, Yessuh, that's our saga. . . . From them cats back in the fields to them cats back in the fields . . . With music and some kind of loud drum beat in the women's walk . . . And so much howl, yeah, that's right, but no weeping, weeping ain't no good. . . . Lemme tell you folks, it's holler you dig, holler and nothing else. . . . Holler Lawd have a mercy, full o' floods and blood and more blues and a heavy hammering, great God that beat in men's lives, them cats loaded with that down home beat in their walk, in their head . . . Whoo mama, who gointer hear that story? Them people just don't want nothin lest it's a joke or a complaint.*

*. . . And don't you know we ain't goin'a clown and*
*we ain't gonna weep either. . . . Just don't want me*
*to put on that holler, them dry Blues, my Lord! . . .*

Is Ken right? Should we forget this? Why is man so
ignorant about what's good for him? Has that white
dream of death and rape covered us all? Have they succeeded in making our whole life a tragedy? Ain't we
kept a health, a coldness through the obscene softening?
A coldness through the fear? What we do. What we do.
What we do. What we do above all. What we do!
Can't you stop that talking machine, that filthy business? What we do! Ain't nothing we do. I don't care.
Stop that shit! Stop wasting your time nigger! Can't
you see you don't make sense, an abstract spook, ain't
even got that thickness them rich white women looking
for a fuck say we got, black nobody drowned in his
own words! A pretty uncool life man! A real square
talk! Git back in. Down in that warm blind egg. There.
Sit down babe, make yourself at home. As long as you
don't get out, ain't nobody goin'a do you no harm.
Ain't no harm they can do you gonna feel. There,
take it easy, take it cool, just sit down. There you is
man, nice, nice, ain't you nice now? No loud square
talk. Warm now. Warm. Hell is comfortable. Hell is
easy. Dig it man, cast down your bucket where you are!

One evening in a little restaurant in Paris, some of those cheap places in Montmartre. He was with a French girl and they were talking French. He used to talk good French. He liked the language. The girl was nice, he liked her allright. They had eaten some French fries and they were ready to go, just sitting there talking French, when two young Americans, a boy and a girl, tall, white and nice-looking, came in. He was there, talking to the French girl in her language. The kid probably thought he was a French West Indian and said, very calmly, aloud, with the detachment of one who is sure not to be understood:

"Hey, darky!"

He was there, talking to the nice French girl and the man was sitting down. He had heard and he hadn't moved. The seconds were passing and nothing happened in him, he was simply thinking: I have heard something he didn't say. That's not what he said, maybe he was talking to the dog, maybe he said, hey doggy, and yet he knew it didn't make sense, but he was thinking the man hadn't said it; just because he had said it with so much coolness, and so gently, and so coldly, with such a lack of excitement, also maybe because that girl was nice and French and he liked her allright. They kept talking as though he hadn't heard, as though he actually didn't understand English and he hadn't understood what the man had said. Minutes had passed and he had known it would be too late to do anything and he had kept on thinking, this is not what he said, I know he didn't say that, and they went out of the restaurant and later that night he had flipped, because he suddenly remembered the voice: he was sure then of what the man had said, he could hear it in his mind and he decided: I'll go find that sonofabitch and cut his throat before he can tell anybody he cursed me out and I didn't move. That night he had run all over Montmartre and Pigalle looking for the man, and he hadn't found him; but he had found another one and that's when he'd cut the white G.I.'s face.

Did Ken take that into account?

How the world are we goin to get out of such a nightmare? What if we keep cutting each other's faces without ever cutting those that should be cut?

Life must be something more real than that. There must be a hole in that curtain of dream through which one could go and start to breathe. How many centuries had people been pressed upon in that way? Pressed upon so they came to believe the point of life was to swing, was to make hell exciting. Closed eyes, and beyond the wave of red or green or blue or yellow light going through the eyelids, streets and avenues and paths and faces and hours, memory of hours, terrible memory of six-thirty in the evening in Charles Street in winter, memory of dawn in Harlem, raining dawn, memory of stores lighting up their windows, of buses waiting for street lights, of Jazz clubs early in the morning with the musicians looking for someplace else where to go, memory, damn full memory of life and sleep and hunger and loneliness . . .

To see Mary . . . To see Mary . . . To see . . . He feels it now with a sudden and strange urgency. To see Mary, right now. Like it can't wait, as though there was not a minute he could lose. He walks in. Richie is not there, though the bar is pretty crowded; he walks through the people. Voices, loud, with a kind of endless wave of laughter and bitterness in them. He walks up to his room, I want to see Mary right now, and stops in front of his door. It's open, there must be somebody inside. He can see a ray of light barring the floor at his feet. Somebody inside. He keeps standing there, in front of the door, thinking it might be somebody to arrest him, or anything like that. I don't give a damn, he whispers. There is the stubborn image of a car, door wide-opened, that sweeps the side of the road, two blond joyful kids. . . . He opens the door.

Mary is in bed, sleeping. He closes the door, switches off the light and lies down beside her. Her body is soft, warm. Lord, so warm!

She wakes up. There is a dark light coming into the room by the half-opened window. The evening, and electric lights all round the house. He can feel that terrible hour, nightfall, and something in his chest gets tight, stiff. She looks at him silently.

"Dan . . ."

"Yeah, baby. Don't move, don't say a word. Here I am, baby, don't talk."

They look into each other's eyes, and there is a quick smile going from his glance to hers. She puts her face against his neck. Mary, Mary, he wants to howl, oh Mary, I just wanted to see you, to hold you, so much! He tries to swallow up the bullet of glue mounting in his throat. Mary!

"I looked for you Dan. All day."

"Keep cool my baby, don't worry. . . ."

"What happened Dan?"

"Nothin . . . I hadda go somewhere. Now it's all checked up. Closed. I done done what I wanted to do. I know what I was lookin for."

He looked at her. Does she know about the bread? Maybe she knows, but she doesn't want to talk about it. Maybe she won't notice it, she'll think she left it somewhere else, or she didn't have it this morning. He watches her soft moves, the slow motion of her body toward his. She is nice. I am not gonna leave her. I am not gonna let her go. I'll keep her with me, he thinks. All the time. He takes her face into his hands, and slowly kisses her mouth. They lie on the bed, both looking at the ceiling, motionless. They don't talk. Good. That's so much taken, so much put apart, that ain't nobody goin'a wreck, nobody gonna steal. Our life, he whispers. That part of our lives they can't control . . .

"Tell me Dan."

He flips. He looks at her, like scared.

"Tell you what?"

"Tell me what it is you think of, what you think, all that."

"Ain't no big thing baby, nothin big really. . . ."

"Hmmm Hmmm . . ."

She kisses him now. He must tell her.

"Listen Mary . . . Maybe you gonna think it don't make sense, but . . . I thought, maybe . . ."

"What?"

"I thought maybe you could stay . . . I mean we could stay together. . . ."

"Ain't we together now?"

"Yeah, sure, but I mean . . ."

"What?"

"Well . . . I don't know how to tell you baby, I mean, I don't want to leave you, I don't want you to go. . . ."

"But Dan, I ain't goin nowhere! I'm here."

"I know, but you don't understand. . . ."

"Yes I understand. I understand allright you want me to be here every day waiting for you to come back and waitin, waitin, waitin all the time, because you don't even know yourself every day whether or not you want to come back. I understand you think maybe if I'd do that, wait for you all the time, every night while you walk somewhere wondering whether or not you'll go home, maybe if I'd do that you'd feel better, 'cause you'd have some girl waitin for you at night, and it'd help you to know how real what you do is. But I tell you Dan, I don't buy that shit. I'm here. You' here too. It's allright; ain't it allright like this? What else you want? You love me and I love you too. But what does it mean? I know men who could kill the woman they loved. I know bitches who really fucked up the man they loved. What you want? Let's not go into all that mess, all that talk. I love you Dan. I love you and I don't give a damn all them words, and that business of stay-together. . . . We ain't got a long life, dig, and them crackers already fuck it up pretty well. Let's not make a mess out of ourselves man! I love you and you say you love me and I'm happy Dan, and all we gotta do is be happy a while, and maybe it'll last, maybe it'll last, maybe it'll last long. . . . But that waitin stuff . . . No man. . . ."

How beautiful she is, he thinks. How beautiful!

They keep lying down, and he bends his head over hers. I love you Mary, he thinks. It's funny, I love you so much. . . . He kisses her mouth, and he feels the stiff bullet of ice in him, the image of two blond-headed killers, and his whole chest is warm, but the bullet doesn't move. Maybe I can love and keep that anger, he thinks. Maybe I can. His hands caress her body, and

**157**

they move, they move as though they were fighting against fever, or a nightmare, they move and he feels her flesh in his hands, her flesh against his, their flesh fighting together. . . .

Lying down. Calm, calm, cool and quiet and slow and fresh and calm. Lying down with the closed circle of a life that slowly folds itself, slowly becomes unreadable. . . . Life like a thick stone, heavy, wordless, life become obvious, maybe become real.

"It's good to be with you Mary. Real good."

"Don't talk Dan. It's good to be here, let's not talk."

Does she know about the twenty bucks? There is a part of herself that knows. I'm sure. Just because she knows me so well. . . . Walkin wonderin whether or not I'll go home . . . Maybe everybody is alike. And we hiding deep down in ourselves things we think are ours, and nobody else's, while everyone got'em.

Europe. It was a Sunday afternoon, he had walked with Nat and his girl in the French countryside and it had started to rain. They'd gone into a forest, and the ground was covered with dead leaves, dead leaves of all colors. Nat was in the Air Force, and he was off every Sunday. They had met somewhere, in a bar or something like that. They used to go out every Sunday, in his car, and they had seen much of the French coun-

158

try that way. The rain had fallen over the dead leaves and the trees were like a roof of branches over their heads. The light was yellow, because of all those leaves and there was no sun, no shade, it was like out of a dream, all they could feel was that deep yellow light rolling upon their eyes. He had told Nat about it, and Nat had looked at him and said:

"You know, it's funny, I felt exactly the same thing, but I thought nobody else would feel it."

"Everybody can feel that, man!"

"Yeah, but dig, you're the first person to ever talk 'bout something like that, to ever talk about what we feel. . . ."

He had known what Nat had said was true. That nobody had ever talked to him about anything but death or gin or sex. And that he had opened a very subtle door in him, just because Nat had always thought that feelings were something more or less shameful, since nobody ever mentioned them.

Life which must stick to the flesh, the rush, the blood.

He gets up. She looks at him.

"You see . . ."

He tightens. Does she try to make him feel guilty or what? What does she mean, saying: you see?

"I see what?"

"Nothin. The reason why I don't want us to get all messed up with them talks. I ain't waitin for nobody, Dan. And I don't expect anybody to wait for me. But this is what men should dig, once for all: that if they feel like being free, or alone, all the time, if they wanna walk all alone and pick up any girl they meet, just like you did with me last night, they'd better not get married. I know you love me Dan, I know it for sure, because I can recognize love, as I know I love you. But you think one can love and remain one, and so do I. And that's why we can't build up no fuckin talk, because we both don't want to accept love for what it is. Maybe because we don't even know why we love. Because it's all we got that's left, all its warmth, pleasure and life . . . Because it's all we got and we don't know anything else."

He looks at her. How does she know that? Where has she learnt? So young and she knows so many answers. Gloria he thinks. Gloria. I shouldn't do that. Try to put faces upon faces, names upon names. People are nothin but themselves, nobody but themselves.

He dresses, a little nervous, something in what she said hit a string in his belly. He doesn't know what, he does not want to know. He walks to her, and they kiss, a long time. "I'll be back later in the night," he says, and she smiles. He walks out of the room. He's mad. He doesn't know why, but he is mad. Real mad.

He is in the bar, looking at the crowd, motionless. He's incapable of moving. Richie walks to him. I hate that smile, that fat warm roar, I can't stand that man. He's a phony. He looks at him, and wonders if Richie ever stops smiling. I'm mad. Lord I'm so mad! Richie keeps smiling his laughter bursts out and covers the bar's noise a minute.

"So, young man, where you been?"

"Nowhere."

"Hmm Hmm! What's the matter? Somethin wrong?"

"Yeah, you goddam right man, somethin's wrong!"

"Ha ha! No big thing, fellow, no big thing. Tell me, tell ol' Richie what's wrong, and we'll fix it up."

Can't that living lie realize he's already dead? Doesn't he know he can't pretend to live like a snake all his life, doesn't he know one morning he'll burst like a balloon, and all that lie he's been will splash all over the place . . .

"No Richie, you ain't goin'a fix nothin! You can't fix nothin! Can you prevent peckerwoods from being what they are? Can you prevent cracker kids from killing niggers? Can you do anything?"

"Oh, I see you goin back on that wrong track agin. Boy, you gotta learn how to get along. How to live with the world."

"Like hell I will! That's a lie, they ain't the world. Why wouldn't they have to git along with us?"

"You crazy, ace, definitely crazy. . . ."

"That might be, I don't know. . . . But I ain't dead yet. Not yet!"

" 'T ain't gonna last too long, the way you go. . . ."

He brutally shakes Richie's big hand and rushes out.

It was in Detroit, just after he had come back from Europe. There were six of them, including a white girl and a young Swiss cat, a Jazz musician. They were in Hastings Street, in the middle of the colored section. They walked calmly, going to he doesn't remember whose house. Just before a street corner, they had seen the crowd. About twelve young Negroes, silent, selling newspapers. Muslim newspapers. They all had realized the danger. They were with a white girl and a white boy, and not only were those two threatened, but all of them were kind of traitors. They had kept walking coolly, as though they had not even noticed the men. The news sellers were like a line across the street and they would have to pass it. There were two or three minutes of terrible tension, while they were getting nearer. Then he had walked out of the group to buy one of the newspapers. While walking toward the men, he flipped. It was Doudou. He had cut his hair, he had gotten older, but it was him. He walked, bought the paper and stayed there, in front of Doudou, wondering whether he could take him into his arms as he would have liked to and looking into Doudou's eyes, waiting for an answer, for a sign. He had smiled, and started:

"Doudou . . ."

"No man!" Doudou's voice was calm, there was no anger, no fear, no resentment. No. Doudou was smiling now, a warm and human smile. "No, don't do that. Go back, man, better go back. Don't let your life be that kind of a drag. Go back."

He had looked at Doudou's calm face, and they had smiled. He would have to go back. Doudou was right. He had walked back to his group, holding the paper in his hand, and they had passed through the line of men. He had kept looking at Doudou, and Doudou was looking at him, still smiling. Later the same night he had realized he hadn't asked Doudou where he could meet him again. And he thought: it's because Doudou knew I would go back, right away, he knew there was no point giving me his address or anything, because I am not going to stay in Detroit. I am not going to stay and he knew it. The day after, he had left Detroit. He was going back down South.

V

That's a bad part of the book. Nothing happens; that talk all the time. A shame; there shouldn't be no talking in a book. Just people who die, kill, love, fight. But who in the world is going to read a book where folks ain't doing nothing but talk and think? LITERATURE! A shame yeah . . .

Maybe it's important too, though. . . .

The big trouble, the bone is somewhere else. Crackers are gonna love that cat, that Peebles. Look, they'll say, ain't he just like we tol' you they are? Dirty and immoral and wanting nothing but money and women, and smoking marijuana, cutting everybody for no reason. . . . You see, ain't nothing we can do with them.

Right. Ain't nothin they're supposed to do either.

Maybe they should better take care of their own selves first. . . .

Switch toward another technique. Don't let a chance for the reader to get used to the tone, to get protected. It's ridiculous in fact, for he's already protected, and no little literary trick is going to put down that barrier of calm and good or bad conscience—which doesn't make much difference anyway. Nothing can compel a man to beware of something he wants to avoid. No song, no howl, no trick. Why write then? . . . Maybe to get one or two weak ones. . . . No. Crackers got a good answer for this too. Let 'em holler they say, it keeps 'em cool. As long as they cry like that, ain't nothing to fear. And then they say, after all, shouldn't they be proud that we hate them so much, that they fill up our lives with so much density? . . . Yeah. . . . But Doudou? What about him? Doudou is a bigger trick. Shouldda written the whole book about him. But nobody would have read it then. It wouldn't provide what it's expected to. Maybe the mere act of writing down something real is a failure in itself. The point is, this is not reality. It's a novel messing around with it. Just touching it sometimes, here and there, cautiously, 'cause it's out of control.

There should be a way of getting to people, though. . . . Some way. But probably not with a book. When I was a kid there was a Blues singer, an old man, and he used to go all over the country, singing, and the words in his songs were like an endless call up to revolt. That was really something. But he was talking to the people. . . . He had no book to write about what happens and how it feels, 'cause the people know. . . . All he did was just call 'em up, better git up now brothers, 'cause who knows whether you'll live tomorrow, that was all he did, just tellin folks we ain't got nothin to lose, so we might as well try any fuckin crazy thing, can't we . . . That's something to be thought of: maybe we shouldn't mess trying to convince anybody. Just talk to people and get 'em up. . . . And this would mean get rid of all that sentimental bullshit we got in ourselves, the habit of crying over our lives when we look at 'em as though we were you, end up that ceaseless game of projection in which everybody finds what everyone looks for. I write about myself for you and I get the exciting feeling, a couple of minutes, that I am you. You read and you think you're Peebles. No more guilt, no more fear, no more disease. Two hours and thirty minutes in your life you've been Peebles: it must give you the right not to be among the privileged. A book is a marvelous machine.

Dig, man, what's the use of all this? Can't you write a book like everybody does, from the start to the end, without having to insert your little personal word here and there, can't you make the novel itself say what you mean? Can't you let that book be a rich vacuum of meaning where we are gonna put what we already know and understand, instead of telling us how to read it and what you mean? We're not interested in what you mean. Less again in what you want us to know.

What are we going to do with Peebles now? Has he got a destiny of his own, does he know inevitability, or is he entirely in my hands, nothing but a character I mold and push and hurt and please and kill as I want? Who can say it? I might not know myself. I can say he is a fiction I control, but how can I know he is not real, whether I am not the one who is being controlled?

Intellectual masturbation. Yet we must try this: to be aware of two or three different levels simultaneously.

We always get back to the same point: if I just sing the Blues, you won't get the message. You'll say it's beautiful and you'll think it's Art. If I don't sing the Blues, if I try to explain, to make you understand, maybe you'll get something out of it, but it won't be the truth, 'cause the bare truth is the Blues. What we think and feel and do is the Blues. And your cecity is such you don't know how to see it. You listen and you say: it's beautiful. It's swinging. It's pure. What to hell can we do? Sing a phony kind of Blues, where the violence, and the horror, and fear would be yours, would be your idea of violence and horror and fear. That's how commercial music was born. That's how work songs became sweet ballads talking about slavery. Because several generations of naive folks thought everything would change if you could understand!

But how could you know that? How could you imagine, not even the fear, not the death or the anger, but how could you imagine that dreadful limitation? That all this violence and all that passivity is a whole universe in itself, within which people spend their whole life, never knowing anything else . . .

Forget it, man! One more time ain't nothin to do on that level. Just blow. We'll see later. Just blow now, and watch my man Peebles running toward something he doesn't know, and nobody knows, but running there sure. . . . That's what happens when one blows. Ain't nobody what knows what's gonna be played but everybody can swear the Lawd it'll unfold and unfold until it gets to an unavoidable end. And no hole, no crack, no silence before that end. The silence of the horn is just a silence of the horn, the breath of the line, and the rhythm section keeps filling up the time all way long. Just a breath of the line. That's what we're at. When the horn stops its line for a couple of bars, to let one hear that rhythmic voice a while. That string

**171**

of rhythm and sheer number that was being played all the time, but which the horn covered.

The big thing is: when twenty million folks are forced to lead an impossible life, to live an impossible situation for more than three hundred years, many of 'em spontaneously become metaphysicians. It's all they can do. And what the hell do you want to do with metaphysicians? They ain't interested in nothing like an actual change, for they're used to looking for different satisfactions. And it don't mean they're happy, or they like it that way. Only, they react and conceive their own situation from the peculiar standpoint of the metaphysician. It implies a certain quality of disaffiliation, it means that passions and will get displaced on another level. Only, not everybody becomes a metaphysician. Many people ain't got a chance to, busy as they are looking for a way of surviving. And that's a real drag, for those ones are incapable of having a ball. And yessuh, that's the very bad thing about it, they dare being dissatisfied. Ain't that a bitch? That's a shame yeah! Something in the system didn't work fine. Unachieved digestion.

Let's not lose that beat. It's about the only way of keeping in touch with a wordless reality. What some call God. That rhythm, that beat is the link.

Now dig, reader, don't forget who you are, who I am, and that Peebles is a paper character. Take it as paper, and if you want to know more about it, if you want to beware the man behind the sign, you'll have to go beyond Peebles, for he ain't but an image, he ain't but a virtual man. Beat is the bridge, the link for that change of world, you just take the risk of being involved in the pyramid of the beat, you just take the risk of assuming communication. Man is behind. But it's a fuckin big risk, man!

Cotton. Back in the belly's rush, the hot taste of cotton. A long and thin song crawls under the walk. Evening. All over the street, the heavy jubilation of evening. People walk: all their lives people keep walking in the streets, going somewhere, coming from some other place and going back, people out in the streets, and that's what makes man's life, this walking, all the time in the same street, everybody. . . . Crowds, crowds, and they talk and they never wonder why they gotta be there, all around the same lousy block of old houses, why they're not alone in the fields or in the woods like rabbits or snakes. Think it's natural, it's the way it gotta work, but they slowly unlearn how to relate to people. Maybe black belts are among the few places in the

174

world where people still know how to relate to people. . . . But that's doubtful too. . . . Maybe it's not that men have forgotten, maybe they never knew, and this science of communication has to be invented! Fuck that crappy business of us having kept some kind of old lousy innocence and simplicity! We're full of their sickness, of all their neuroses. . . .

\*

\*    \*

Daniel Peebles went out of Richie's, gave the noisy street a short look, and started walking toward the bus stop. He was going slowly, as though absorbed in a deep meditation. The night was falling rapidly, lights were shining here and there. After five minutes, Daniel Peebles arrived at the bus stop. There was a bench above which there was a sign saying: COLORED. A few feet further, there was another bench, bigger and newly painted, saying: WHITE. He sat down on the first bench, very calm, his face did not move at all. It was like a man with no expression. He had crossed his legs, and there was something slightly comic about the elegance of the gesture beside the filth of the bench.

Twenty minutes passed. Daniel Peebles was still

sitting on the bench, under the sign. He had not moved. Slowly he uncrossed his legs, looking at them with what looked like a deep interest. Then he turned his head and looked at the clock behind him. It showed 7:30. Night had fallen now, completely. He was very quiet. Obviously he was very quiet. A man came and sat at his side. He was an old man, maybe not very old, but very tired, and poorly dressed, with pants too wide and too long for him. The man looked at Peebles, still staring at the night right in front of him.

"The bus ain't goin'a be here before one hour, boy! We gotta wait a mighty long time. . . ."

The old man looked at Peebles, expecting an answer, but no answer came. Daniel Peebles seemed not to have heard. The man coughed noisily two or three times, to signify his presence. Peebles looked at him and there was still no expression on his face. He opened his mouth to talk, but no muscle in his eyes flipped. There was a kind of stoned fixity in his glance.

"You're right, that's a mighty long time."

His tone was cold, there was no passion, no life in his words. He added:

"But you're used to waitin, and so am I, ain't we?"

"Well . . . You the young'uns should know better'n wait. Let the crazy ol' things like me wait. But you got too much time before you to waste it waitin for a bus that might never come!"

Daniel Peebles did not answer. He just nodded his

head, and the old man could not tell whether that meant an agreement or not. Peebles had started looking in front of him again. Then he talked, but he did not seem to care about being heard by the old man. His cold and quiet voice rose, and he talked slowly, sounding as if he was not sure himself of what he said.

"Perhaps one man's destiny, only one man's, is not all that important. It's not all that big a thing."

His hand went deep into his pocket and came out with the marijuana cigarette he had saved that morning. He showed it to the old man.

"Know what this is?"

The man saw the thin cigarette and he looked at Peebles in horror.

"You . . . You . . ." His voice was burning with indignation. "You . . . you're not gonna smoke that here . . ."

"You don't want to get high?"

The old man seemed really outraged. Outraged and scared at the same time. He got up, and looked for something to say, he seemed very angry. Daniel Peebles got up too and put his hands upon the old man's shoulders, pushing him back on the bench.

"Keep sittin down here daddy. . . . Don't worry, I am not going to smoke it here. I'll come back."

And he walked away from the old man, in the direction of the countryside.

He walked a few steps and stopped. He took a match-

**177**

box out of his left pocket and lighted the cigarette. He breathed the smoke. He walked back toward the street, still holding the cigarette between his lips and breathing the smoke every now and then. He passed before the bus stop, the old man was sitting on the bench, he had gotten an old paper out of his pocket and he was reading. He saw Peebles walking in the middle of the street with the stick in his mouth, and he immediately plunged his face in his paper in sign of protest. Daniel Peebles laughed. There were people walking around him and no one seemed to notice the cigarette, in spite of the smoke's sweet smell. He noticed a man standing before a door. It was the same man he had met the night before with Mary. Chuck she had said. He walked to him. Chuck saw him and laughed.

"Hey daddy? Feel better?" Then he saw the stick and burst out in laughter. "Oh man! I swear the Lawd you' fresh! gitt'n high right here in the middle of town at seven o'clock. . . . Ain't you ever doin nothin but gittin high?"

"Oh yeah . . . A whole lotta things, but right now I'm in a smokin mood. So I just smoke, 'cause I'm free. We're all free. Why wouldn't we do what we please?"

Chuck looked at him intently. Peebles caught his arm and said:

"Dig brer, look-a-here, I wanna show you somethin. Come an' walk with me."

Chuck nodded his head. There was an expression of amused distrust painted on his face.

**178**

"Okay daddy'o, let's go and see."

They walked toward the bus stop. The old man, still drowned in his paper, did not seem to even notice them. Peebles was still breathing the smoke, and Chuck looked at him.

"After all, you're right, daddy'o, fresh enough to smoke in town with all the folks around, and ain't nobody sayin nothin. They's just so sure it's impossible, they don't believe it when it's under their eyes."

They had stopped in front of the bench, a few steps away from the old man. Daniel Peebles indicated the sign with his finger and said:

"See that sign there? It gave me an idea."

"Ho ho! Let's hear that!"

"Well you see . . . We just go git ourselves a big sign like that, a big sign written: COLORED, one to a person, everybody, and we walks in town carryin'em around. Just walkin with that big old sign above our heads, sayin, COLORED, and couldn't nobody say nothin, 'cause ain't it just what they want? That we keep our place like they say . . . Just they think we don't need no goddam sign, 'cause it's pretty obvious that we's black, but with them signs above us, ain't no peckerwood gonna sit on none of us. Ain't even gonna touch us, that'd be against their laws!"

There was a rhythmic softness in his voice now. Chuck looked at him and burst out again.

"You're crazy man! Why to hell are you such a crazy motherfucker?" He was laughing, and Peebles started laughing too, and they were both laughin like mad, right in front of the serious and outraged little man. Peebles looked at Chuck and touched his arm.

"Dig . . ."

"What?" Chuck asked. "You too high man!"

"I ain't high!"

"You're crazy then!"

They both started laughin again, clapping each other's hand. Peebles tried to stop laughin and said:

"No, but dig, man, you gotta watch them signs. . . . We's very hip about signs. . . . Like a cat told me once . . . Just imagine what would happen if the people go to a Ku-Klux Klan meeting, you dig, they jus' go there . . ."

"Yeah, so what? . . ."

"Well, they just go there you see, and all the Klansmen they take off them masks you see . . ."

"Unh nnh . . ."

"They take off their masks, and they're all spades!"

Daniel Peebles burst out laughing. Chuck looked at him with a kind of bitter smile, and tried to laugh.

"You're completely nuts man!"

They went back toward the bar, silently. After a few steps Chuck turned toward Peebles and looked at him, smiling. They had stopped. Chuck's smile was sad and warm. He put his arm over Dan's shoulder and said:

"You goin through hell ain't you?"

"Yeah, maybe. . . ."

"You can't live like that, brother. . . . Not with them jokes about the Klan and gitt'n high in the middle of the street. You gotta do some'n about yourself."

Peebles didn't answer. Chuck kept talking.

"How long you been back here?"

"How you know I am back?"

"I know you from here, 'cause of the way you talk and all that. And I know you've been away, 'cause you wouldn't have cracked that joke about the Klansmen. . . ."

"I been back about a month."

"And you ain't gotten in no trouble yet? Man, you lucky!"

Daniel Peebles kept silent.

\*

\*     \*

Yeah, that kind of crackin up is impossible here. That's proved. I can't be free here, no matter what I do or think. However free I feel. I just can't have that freedom pass into life, pass into people. I can deceive myself so I won't care sitting under a sign, but I can't help the fact I do have to sit there. And it's true that such a joke can't be funny HERE! Maybe I am not capa-

181

ble of remaining what I have become, if I stay here. Maybe I'll have to switch back to somebody I have been a long time ago. . . . No! Not with what I learnt in the last four days. This is something I can't lose. I've just been a fool thinking what I just did could be an answer. It's funny how two hours of a life can be just a step backwards, a hole, and we gotta start back to hours before.

He felt Chuck's arm over his shoulder. He liked Chuck. It would be hard to say why but he liked him. Chuck was talking, talking about that kind of life not being possible, and he should find a way . . .

"Let's go back to the bus stop, Chuck. I wanna see if I go tonight."

"Where?"

"Anywhere. I just want to go. Maybe I'll go back up North. Ain't got enough bread to get there, but I'll work that out."

"Maybe that's the best you can do. Ain't no means for you of staying here, you gotta learn again too much. I can stay here because my whole life's already fucked up. Couldn't do nothin with it. The young folks they stay here too, 'cause they tryin'a do somethin about what happens. They's swingin, I mean, I dig what they do. . . . But you can't stay man! You won't last enough to get as fucked up as me, and you won't know how to live like the young'uns goin'a sit in a Jim Crow lunch counter and wait for the cops to bus you, and call that a fight. You won't know how to do that. . . ."

"Yeah. . . . Maybe I don't even want to. . . . You really think that's a fight?"

"No. But what else you know?"

"There must be somethin to do, for you and me, and so many. . . . Somethin more real than all them sit-ins. I mean, sit-ins are very good, but we're in a fuckin rush man! We ain't got three more hundred years to wait. Maybe there's a means for us to get up, you know, just get up and not let nobody fuck with us, whatever we have to fear. . . ."

"Yeah . . ." Chuck talked slowly, he was staring at the sidewalk, thinkful. "Yeah . . . I think of it sometimes. I heard them cats, the Muslims, two or three times. But folks don't want to change that much. I'm tellin you, brer, them kids is really cool, but they ask too much of the people. . . . I mean, like they want a real change. . . ."

"Don't you want a real change?"

"Yeah, but it's hard. Get rid of all you know, all you have, even when all you know is bullshit and all you have is ass-kicking."

He had thrown the roach away. He was not high. Not really. He was only a little more present, he stuck to the time a little more, but he was not high. They arrived at the bus stop. When he saw them, the little old man got up and went to sit on the sidewalk, a few steps farther. They sat down on the bench.

Fear. Cotton and ice. It had been like a game, that hour. Real ice with the old man, but it had started to melt away when he'd met Chuck. Or maybe it was the stick. Now he was sitting on the bench again, but he had lost the heaviness, the stiffness. . . . That's better, he thought. It was a mistake. The night in front of him. Houses like vague shadowy shapes in the dark blue. Lights a thin string of yellow stars covering the night like a net. Fear, the same good old one, widening in his body, and he doesn't even feel it any longer. Fear become intimate part of his blood and breath. Fear come back. But he hasn't forgotten anything. Man is being built up, stone after stone, brick upon brick. He looks at Chuck. Yeah, there must be a way. I can have Doudou grow on that earth.

Chuck was staring at the ground, and there was a kind of childish expression behind the rough-looking face. His voice rose, and it had lost its bitterness, its violence, its brutality.

"You know . . . I ain't done nothin with that messed up life of mine. Just stealin and impin and hustlin and cuttin too, sometimes, not too much. . . . And I never liked it. I ain't kiddin, man, or tryin'a say I'm a good little family boy, but the choice was too bad a bargain. I seen men who tried to be honest, here, really they tried,

I seen them. It didn't help 'em none. Nohow. They'd get killed and spat upon and kicked in the ass and cursed out just like anyone else. I don't mean they were wrong, but I can't accept it for myself, I can't take it. I am no fuckin lamb. . . . But now I can see them years pass behind me and I know I ain't gotten nowhere either. Just sometimes I wish I'd do a thing to be a man, anything. . . ." His voice got louder. "Mebbe one day ahma git me a gun and shoot me somebody. . . . Shoot me a couple o' crackers and knock my own head out then. That wouldn't be too bad a death. I think I wouldn't care dyin if I'd done that before. I know a guy who done it. He'd taken his car and he'd gone to the white neighborhood; then he'd started runnin over people and he'd killed two or three of 'em when they took him. And when they got to the 'chine he was dead, with a big hole in his head and a gun in his hand." He stopped a while. His voice became low again. "That is no bad death. It's better'n hunger or shame. . . ."

"Yeah, I think I know what you mean." Dan thought: so much to rectify, so much to undo. What would Doudou think of Chuck? And he knew Chuck was sincere, saying he'd do that one day.

Walk. The world is becoming wet, my hand, wet on Chuck's wet shoulder, that fuckin endless walk among the wet walls. I dig Chuck. I know what he means. So

**185**

damn well, I know what he's got to live with, that bright knowledge of death coming near. . . . Lord, it's amazing how man can be one whole thing, just the very same all the time, like something that would keep happening the same way, endlessly, some kind of endless Jazz. Yet anything is possible. People are free, but maybe that's too much to beware. People happening like chords, however peculiar they wanna be, incapable of not being helplessly related to people! Some day Chuck would get hisself a gun and shoot a sonofabitch or two. That would be one more, or one first black dream made death, made real death with blood and pain, and no fear, no more fear. . . . Can one say a nightmare is the end of a dream? Why are we sentenced to that murderous nonsense of a life, why can't we see the essential anywhere but in that rotten business of death and anger?

He stopped. Chuck looked at him.

"What's the matter?"

"Nothin man. I'm thinking I'm goin'a leave the South again and I know it'll be soon."

"I done tol' you that's about the best you can do."

Now they were walking again.

Go somewhere else. Start again maybe, the same crappy old groove. No, not with what I know now. Not with what I learnt. It's a wild situation: that I have to decide about what my life is going to be as though I had no past, no limitation at all! Go back up North, yeah, maybe go back up there and try to work my way out toward something cleaner. He felt Chuck's thick presence at his side, and he thought: his too. His life too, that's been switching from purity and pride to nightmare and filth. How will I think of this period I am living now after ten years? Will I even? He couldn't imagine it. It'll probably seem much worse than what it actually means to me. It'll probably look like I was really catching hell. . . . Funny!

"Look man, I'm thirsty as hell. Let's go somewhere and drink some. . . ." Chuck looked at him, smiled and said:

"Okay. Let's go to my place then. I got a couple o'bottles home. Good bourbon."

"Hunh hunh! Bourbon! That's somethin else!"

They walked. Chuck didn't live very far. It was almost out of town, after the bus stop, in a little unlighted street. He opened a wooden door and they were in. One single room, but clean enough. Pictures on the walls: movie stars, Jazzmen, half-nude colored women. In the army he thought, the women in the pictures were white. But indeed, this is in Mississippi. They sat down on the bed and Chuck took a bottle from behind a pile of magazines, opened it and gave it to him. He put the bottle to his lips and started drinking. He didn't like that. Actually, he didn't like any alcohol, whether it was bourbon or gin or anything. But he used to drink

187

pretty much, just to be like everyone else. The spirit burned his throat, tears almost came to his eyes. He gave the bottle back to Chuck.

"Been livin alone all the time?"

"No. . . ." Chuck's voice seemed to hesitate. . . . "No . . . I was married once. 'T didn't work. Had a house in the country, that is, a big cabin, and chickens and all that. Fine time. Didn't work, that's all."

They kept silent. What the world am I doin here? Why is it that I am here, back in Mississippi, and this room looks like something I know, I didn't know people could live here as though they were in Chicago or New York. . . .

Night. Cold columns of night around this small coin of living warmth. The same old known song all through the night. I shouldn't let myself go to that sort of softening, maybe it's the church's heritage coming back. The feeling of the sacred, everything is holy, my ass like a prayer, yeah, maybe that's my whole life getting opened to some bigger sight: people that have been made things, shining and metallic, and that poor old motherfucker still looking for some lost and innocent ground, the softness of a naked member, the beat in that night.

Church . . . Yeah, maybe there had been something in that too. Not only the same amazing hypocrisy of my uncle. There must have been something else. Something that also had to do with jubilation, like sharing

**188**

in a big secret, there was a funny feeling of nudity, as one being endlessly watched. . . . How would it be possible to unmix it from the bullshit?

He looked at Chuck. Yeah, he's probably right when he say he done messed up his life. But what else could be done? How? Life that feverishly becomes a forest of questions, and man getting every time a little farther from his own reality. Man getting lost. Mute. He keeps looking at Chuck, and they drink again, that's a pretty swingin little room, he says, aloud, and Chuck laughs, softly, as not to break the stuff of time being made. Nothing happens. One more hole, he thinks, and nothing happens. Once my life used to be full of time, no holes, something always happened. But maybe that's because I actually thought everything took place within one's own mind. There couldn't be no holes.

"I am gointer go now. . . ."
"Keep cool daddy, no rush, you can stay a lil' more."
"No, really man, I gotta go."

He was a little drunk. Funny, he hadn't been high while smoking, but now, with those two nips of bourbon, he was gone. It's crazy, how easily I can be out of what I'm livin and look at it as though it wan't myself. Maybe that's what happens to those who have to dream all their life, in order not to see the shit under their own feet. He got up and walked to the door, thinkin: I am goin to go and see Mary again. And then: it's crazy how that girl's been filling up my life for two days and I just can't imagine my life without her now.

"Chuck?"

"Yeah. . . ."

"Dig man, I probably never see you again, 'cause I'm leavin for good. But take it easy brer, make yourself a good time if you can. I'll remember you, that you can be sure. I ain't goin'a forget nothin. . . ."

"Cool daddy'o, cool. . . . I won't fergit you either. Take good care of yourself!"

Their hands clasped, and they were like laughin, but there was a sort of soft crying in that laughter. He opened the door, and the street jumped to his face, the whole crowded warmth of the sidewalks just widened in front of him, around him. He walked out.

"Can you find your way back?"

"Don't worry brother, I'll make it. Thanks. Bye!"

One more brother left behind. One more man gone, and nothing but memory to stick to his lost warmth and love. Get back to the walk. . . . I wish Mary is home now. He smiled, because he had thought of Richie's as his "home." Ain't that somethin? He almost runs toward the lighted street. Funnily vague images go through his mind. He whispers slowly, Mary, Mary. . . . It's pretty good to pronounce the name just like that, like chewing the very sign of a presence. He is out there in the street, the main lighted street, walking quickly but steadily toward the bar and Richie and Mary, maybe, Mary! . . .

I love her he thought. I sure do. I must be a pretty ridiculous show, crazy old sonofabitch falling in love like I am fourteen or some. . . . That's a whole lotta crap too, he whispers, maybe I've never been so able to love as now. Why the hell would I bother thinkin it might look funny or anything, ain't Richie said that was my life and that's the only thing he said that made sense, ain't I the only one that can say a word about it?"

He is almost in front of the door. It is probably about nine.

I don't know anything. I don't know nothing. Get back there, to the hot anguish of ignorance. Drop it, drop that walk, that endless fight and tension, it's just so damn hard to be an adult all the time. Get high to escape. . . . No, even that's too hard. What if I were wrong, what if the world could not be changed, if all I had to do was to do what I please, whatever the neighbor will have to pay for it. . . . He heard Chuck again: people don't want to change that much! How was that? How had people gotten chained in what they used to be so that they became incapable of shaking the whole goddam world off its filth? I know nothing. I might be a poor fool. Chuck might be a fool to think he's been wrong, living the way he did. Can people, a whole people be wrong? It sounds crazy, but still . . .

Defeat has been there, along his walk, along every step of his song, warm and tempting. Soft and obscene like my uncle's lousy God. All I know is Mary. I am not fit to make my whole life sound like a nice story. All I know is Mary, her skin and her mouth. All else is empty words. I have been too far in mess, I've been too fucked up to even feel any other pain and revolt. Only Mary. I couldn't live in another world either, just like Ken or Chuck. I'd think it's no fun, or some shit like that. . . . Maybe that's where their very crime lies: our being tied to the death of their sinking boat! I gotta sleep. That's what. When I wake up all'll be different, all is goin to be better-looking, cleaner-looking.

He hasn't moved. Time hasn't moved. As though time and life were going along different beats, different speeds.

I gotta see Mary before I go. What she has to say will decide about what I'll do, but she won't know how heavy her words will be, she'll just blow, not knowing she is being recorded, not knowing how much flesh and breath is involved in her words.

He walks into the bar.

# VI

Reckon a little rupture wouldn't be too bad. Something like a break in the timetable. Just conventional flash-backing. One gets tired of following Dan Peebles step after step, every damn minute of his poor journey. We'll take it back a little later. Of course, it's only a phony trick, for what we'll miss is probably not that important. Besides, it's an annoying part to write. But I keep saying the point is to avoid monotony.

Is the journal true? Is it really a journal somebody wrote without any literary intention and upon which I would have built up the novel? Or is the whole thing, journal included, a mere fiction? Did I write the journal? Was it actually my journal, did I write it on purpose, did somebody else write it? That's a question to be thought of. No kidding, that's a question that might make sense! The point is: what goddamn difference can it make anyhow? Ain't the whole thing one same nightmare?. . . Unh unh! I'm not that sure it don't make no difference. It shouldn't, but people look for slices of life, for documents. I mean that's what they claim they want. In fact, they don't really want 'em, for whenever they fall upon one, they yell in horror; what they actually dig is Art: it can't concern but one's mind, it ain't but Art, it doesn't necessarily involve consciousness. But now the fashion is for Art to be made an ersatz of something real, of the image of something real. . . . It's too damn complicated! And it can't even be made a general rule. . . . A drag!

Let's let Peebles talk again. As we know he's goin to die, if HE talks about it it'll be obvious, at last, that he didn't write it, it'll look more like a novel. But you know, the doubt will remain there anyway: how much of it is true? How much of it is for real?

Other reasons too . . . Inner construction of the book. Novel framed by a journal and a monologue.

That's about all I should have to say. Now Dan's going to take it. Whatever has to be said he'll say. We're two different persons though. . . . Proof: I'm still alive.

Proof that the last part, at least, can't be an autobiography!

All that becomes secondary. . . . Now the center switches back on Peebles' talk, and not over our mental bullshit any longer. Maybe now the story can talk for itself. All I can do is try. Just try and blow.

Ladies and gentlemen, thank you for your attention. Our show begins.

Don't forget this ain't but a show. Keep looking at the door in the theater, the curtain and the ceiling for the open-air scenes, all the details to which you'll have to stick, in order to remain quite lucid about the characters being actors playing characters representing people.

Please, Sir, don't forget.

Half of myself thinks it's better to play upon your guilt feelings than to blow away their reasons as well as them. This might be a key. But what's the best, on the level of efficiency, and how much guilt do you have that can be played upon? It varies with individuals. . . . Ain't nobody that knows for real. And then, isn't it a wrong level to put the point on? Ain't reality involved with colder, more actual problems? More actual than guilt, anyway? Let's forget it. All to be done don't depend on words.

Sand. Slowly the night's string gets torn. That's longer burning of the dark, shorter breath. Sand, red under the dust, heavy as our hopes. I am afraid to see the soft darkness break, afraid to see the darkness split.

I knew it would get back to that runaway. Maybe ahma die. That would be damn silly. Still, I might have to get used to the idea, and quickly. Maybe ahma die today. Things seemed to start workin fine though. . . . A room, a girl, and then whooo! All way down! Maybe ahma die today, and it's funny, ain't it, but I can't feel it that much, it's such a common scene in my mind, so well known! . . .

What I'd like to understand is what happened with

Mary. It's been that which started it all. Now, they're after me. Ain't got too much time to think about it. . . . Anyway, it's always the same story, everybody knows that scheme, it's even amazing that it keeps happening that way, used up as the process is. But maybe crackers can't be conscious of such subtleties. They're more concerned with the blood than with the way it bleeds.

Morning, carrying its load of stones in the heads. Morning, when the glance sinks and gets lost, sinks and unfolds. She wasn't home when I got back. Gone. Gone one more time. Ain't nothin to hold against her. Can't keep people. Gotta know how to. Shouldn't be that hard, but maybe it is. He suddenly flips, because a terrible thought crosses his mind. Then he whispers no, I am sure she didn't leave because of the twenty bucks. But he knows it's too late, he shouldn't have thought of it, now that thought is going to remain, entire, in a small corner of his head, and he'll never be able to get rid of it completely.

No time for cryin. Maybe ahma die today, I know they'll find me if they want to, ain't no spook down here escaped scotfree after hitting a cop. Gotta be mad to do it anyway! But Richie is still wrong though: beautiful world that taught us how precious life was while killing us little by little. It's one man's own choice to decide whether certain things can be more precious than life. Only thing Richie said that was true:

one's own life: can do whatever he wants with it. Wreck it up if that's what he likes.

It's early in the morning. Flat, not hot yet. He has not slept, his mouth tastes like dirty cotton, and he is hot. I am tired. Lord, very tired.

Crazy: death is not that solemn, for one can't ever see it all in front, embrace all it means at once. All it doesn't mean. But it's like a phony feeling: be able to look at my life as though it were ended, but be incapable of realizing it's actually almost ended. It sounds like a big joke. I just can't believe it. Never has my life seemed more unreal to me as now. I am completely alien.

Maybe what it means is life coming back in waves of hot breath. And breaking the stuff of anguish in the belly. Waves with all their smells, their light, their taste, waves filled with all our frightening love for life . . . Warm waves blown over the face, and that's a very cold and healthy fright coming down on me. Strong and loud, nothing to see with the too well-known fear.

She was gone. Hadn't left no letter, for maybe she didn't write too well. She'd just told Richie she'd thought us over and she'd thought it'd be better for the both of us to part. To part after one night! Same old jazz happening the same way all the time. . . . But maybe I'm wrong thinking that was the reason. Maybe it was something else, maybe it was . . . Shit! We should get used to putting our problems on a higher level, since they actually are.

I hit the cop because I wanted this to happen. I hit the cop because he was ugly. I hit the cop because he was there when I got there. I hit the cop because he flipped when he saw me. I hit the cop because she was gone. I hit the cop because he secretly wanted me to. I hit the cop because he was afraid. I hit the cop because he was white and something about white people makes me mad because I know I can't be myself in front of them. I hit the cop because he was a white cop in Mississippi, the most taboo animal on the face of America. I hit because all my words, all my intellectual bullshit, my tricks to feel free can't help no boot down here to be free, even one minute, because why we're what it means to be a nigger down South doesn't happen in our minds. I can't blind myself well enough not to see that a white cop is a white cop. What it involves as power and fear and elementary emotions. And I find something obscene in such exhibitions. I hit the cop because I was mad. Because I'm mad. Men made machines, made machines of which the only function is to strike upon men, to beat, to kill men. Men made machines of which the only function is to hate and smile, is to have contempt and envy, is to kill back and cry. I'm mad, sure yeah, I'm mad all right, if you ain't never seen a mad nigger look at me, I'm mad because ahma die maybe today and I don't know anything, I haven't got nothing out of my life but a few fugitive impressions of nightmare and horror, and I ain't got no message to leave to nobody, no word someone could remember and try to live with. I hit the cop because he was nobody and I knew it was still enough to kill me, maybe because I have kept an insane love for tragedy like somebody who wouldn't know tragedy, and doctors would probably say it's because I never wanted to admit Maurice's death. The big Trauma. The big bullshit. I hit the cop because I loved her and never was I able to love people the way they want to be loved.

I don't know why I hit the cop.

It was in autumn, somewhere in Paris' Left Bank. I had no money, like always, and I passed by one of them sidewalk cafes. Lots of people were sitting there, drinking beer and coffee and things like that. It might have been about five in the afternoon. I stood there, a few steps away from the tables, looking at that beautiful and terrible city, Paris, where one could die starving so easily, looking at its life and fever. There was something like a sheet of coldness being torn up in that glance, letting appear the hot flesh underneath.

What part did the fact that I was black play in my life? That's a jive question to ask in the first place: everything depended on it. Yeah, but I mean, what was the margin of freedom within the conditioning, how large was it?

Am I going to die here, now? I remember how death was always implied, always tacitly involved in every one of our gestures, every one of our words. And the way little things were made dear to us, the way we had to stick to anything, the way we were able to laugh, really lose ourselves in laughter, the way we knew every minute was won against fear and agony. Maybe ain't nobody ever gonna be able to really translate that. Really give it back: the very simple horror and absurdity of being an American Negro. The very need we have to make that situation possible, so that we can find within it enough sense and peace, the very fear we have of seeing the world change, because we've been beaten and fooled so many times that any little thing we have we don't want to lose. Who will ever be able to say that, as simply as a Blues sung by a couple of sharecroppers, and no one among the motherfuckers who pretend to like their singing has ever realized the very dimension of what it meant.

It is nine o'clock in the morning. He's been walking for about one hour. He knows the men after him aren't but five or six. Times done changed. When he was a kid the whole town used to go out hunting niggers. Now there ain't but a few fans left, except for the big occasions. The others just don't give a damn. Anything can happen, they won't move.

I was standing there in front of the cafe and a guy came by and stopped three steps behind me, in front of the people. He had a violin and he got ready to play. I thought: one more student tryin'a make a little money. I looked at him. He didn't look like no beatnik though. He was normally dressed, very clean. I flipped, 'cause he looked American. Something about him. The way he was dressed, and also the way he stood up. He looked Jewish, too. I looked at him with a kind of re-sentment. Something in his bearing made me think he was southern. I whispered: cracker. Cracker sonofa-bitch. Then he started playing. I flipped at the first notes. He could play. Really he could play. I stayed there like stunned. The melody flowed over the street, pure and bare, it was something for violin or cello, but he played it on the violin. Lord, he could play, all right! I was mad at myself, mad at him. Why do crackers play good music too? When he got through—and he didn't seem to care about the people giving him money or not, he just played, closed eyes, on the edge of ecstasy—

when he had finished, I walked to him and I felt slightly ridiculous when I said:

"Great, man, that was great. . . ."

He looked at me with a kind of distrust, as though he thought I was laughing at him. He answered with a Texas accent, and I thought again: why do crackers make beautiful music too?

"Thank you. You like Bach?"

What does he think, because I'm black, I can't dig nothin besides ragtime?

"I don't care whether it's Bach or Julius Caesar, all I know is it's good music."

He'd laughed. I was disturbed by his attitudes. They didn't seem to be any less prejudiced than anybody else's, but the way he lived them was peculiarly cool and natural, I couldn't find any hatred, any fear in him. Later, when we had become friends, I told him one day of my first thought: why do crackers make good music too? He laughed, and he told me he was a Jew. I answered it didn't make any difference to me, and he said it made one to him. He was a little crazy about that, I never really understood. I mean, I knew them cats had had a real rough time, but it didn't mean such a big difference with the other white people in my mind as it did in his. Anyway, he was the one that started complicating everything, for it was hard for me to reckon with the friendship of a white southerner, Jewish or not. But several times I thought: he wouldn't be the same in Texas. He couldn't. I was contented with the thought, because it meant I didn't really have to change anything in my own attitudes. It was only much later that I understood he really considered me as a man, and really as a friend. Much later I understood he had given me a whole lot and I hadn't ever trusted him or felt any deep feeling toward him, because he seemed to share in a world that wasn't mine, for we had been thrown out of it so many times we had gotten into the habit of hating it as a whole.

I am not goina die. I can't believe it. I feel just like every day, I know the cotton in my stomach so well I can't believe I am more in danger now than I ever was.

Life that had been motionless dust in the field's dance, heels made minutes, hard heels in the field's dust. We had seen the insane fears on that bank, our hunger given back to the more essential land of our childhoods. We were rain through hard hands, rain, heavy. Water made rhythm, back made song, yeah there, right there and then we were gestures made dance, motionless hand sticking to the gesture's breaking.

What the fuck did happen when I hit the cop? What in my mind? I must have been high. I thought that was the kind of shit I would stop doing, at least down here. It's funny, I'm still in love with Mary. . . . One man's gonna die loving her. Ain't that a bitch? Reckon I love her because I don't know why she left. Maybe it's true that there are some events in my life I stubbornly refuse to take into account. Just can't admit that they did happen. Keep living as though I didn't know they'd actually taken place.

It must be about nine-thirty now. He walks in the same fields as a week before, but the other way. No big difference. That's probably why he can't realize he's going to die.

Things I always lived with. The very fundamentals of what our life deals with. For centuries we've been trying to make ambiguity sensible to men, and now the time has come to wonder whether it was not a crazy purpose. Whether choice is avoidable . . . If we don't have to get rid of everything that makes us, everything that makes us ourselves in order to get rid of that which poisons our life . . . If all we like, all we feel, is not intimately tied to what we hate, is not linked and part of what we hate . . . Are we sure we don't have to undergo a complete revolution in ourselves and our attitudes if we want to throw away all the bullshit we claim we don't want? Hasn't the white dream of death and rape that's been covering us for centuries rotted every little corner of our lives? How can we know we'd be able to live without what makes our life?—that mixture of dread and dance, the habit of thinking of man who cries is swinging, all that knowledge we have of how things happen in people's minds and of how a man can be led from nowhere to hell without his having to do nothing but let it happen. . . . How can we be sure we don't also have to get rid of that, because it's all been rotted by the same wild scheme of blood and grimace. Is it possible to think of another world, where people would be sane and square? . . . How many of us could answer this? . . . Who in this here world, except crackers who'd yell it goes against nature to even think of it, could answer this: is it possible to think the world can be made into something cleaner, where we'd be free of all sick attitudes, whether they'd be justified or not?

He is still walking. Lord, I'm so tired, I know that slow death of the man who runs so well. I've done that run in mind so many times, Lord, 'cause I'd thought I wouldn't be able to know your real face without knowing how it feels to see death running after you and slowly getting to you. . . .

I liked New York. Winter in Harlem, however hard, there was something about it that made it subtle and burning, yeah, like dawn and the musicians looking for some other place where they could go and listen to some more sounds. That's life coming back, like something I would spit back. The fields all around. Ain't nothin around but them fields all over and the hills, too. . . . Dear Old Southland . . . Dear old Bluesland . . .

Maybe ahma die today. It's a real drag not to have any time to think of it, to realize it and draw up a little balance, look backwards and think: okay, here is what's been done, what's been good, and that didn't work. Just a while to look back and decide what meaning I want to give my death. . . . But those problems are unreal. One man's own life can't be that big a problem. It must not be. But perhaps it's not only mine. . . .

Why the hell did I have to hit that cop? What for?

If I die, it will mean something for twenty million black people. Something good or bad? Maybe papers are gonna talk about it. 'T sounds crazy, for they won't ever know how it really took place, how it happened and what it meant to me. What the hell are we bothering about all that for? Are we gonna change anything with words? Can we . . . ? We ought to be more familiar'n that with death. Ought'a know one man's ain't no big thing, except when it's yours. What's only terrible about it is this fear of dying too soon, without having had the time to think of all. Like one would've like to say: okay, now I'm ready, when I say GO! start it. Not before. I am desperately looking for a solemnity of some kind, and all I can find is that filthy increasing fear in my chest, in my belly.

Morning. Naked one more time. Dry morning. He's not going to cry. That he knows. There's been too much crying, too much emphasis in his life. Now he's dry. Almost completely dry . . . Looking for some beautiful speech to deliver before splitting the scene, and knowing that won't happen. There ain't gonna be no speech, 'cause people just don't die that way, 'xcept in movies.

Why the fuck did I have to hit that cop?

Gloria. Mary. I was married once. Would I have started it all again with Mary? Now all that's past, all that's one more bunch of dead black dreams. I shouldn't be terrified by death. Not with what I've seen. Korea. Waking up one morning and seeing clearly all that blood and murder. Wondering: in the name of what? For who? . . . Discovering: I am not the murderer, but something worse: his accomplice. Because I'm black and that fight can't be mine. And maybe the Korean's is mine. Finding back: guilt, guilt, guilt, GUILT! What I am living right now is nothing next to that. What I'm living now already belongs to a world that's been condemned to death. That was condemned to death the very day it was born. But that very trap of blood where man fell. All that blood to undo . . . Maybe the very strength of Doudou came from this: he was not controlled by individual sensitivity any longer. He'd become aware of bigger, larger realities. Maybe he knew what "society" means, what it is and how it works. . . . Maybe it's what we lack, what's killing me. That ignorance, that incapacity for replacing our small bloody conflicts within a whole, that incapacity for giving them a sense.

He is slowly running among the fields. Suddenly, he stops. What am I doing? What do I hope, running like that? I sure must be crazy! They gonna get me anyway if they want. I'd better try to hide out somewhere. Pearl. He thinks of Pearl's cabin all of a sudden. That's not too far, he thinks. That's the best I can do. Just try to get there before they get to me and maybe her man will find something. . . . He takes on his right, running a little faster. He can hardly breathe now, for he's really running, he can feel all the blood beating in his chest, in his head. He doesn't think of anything any longer, but of Pearl's cabin, as though it were really a safe place, not wanting to be aware of the whole absurdity of the run, its air of a sad joke.

Ahma die today. I know. Lord! We just ain't said nothin. We just ain't known nothin of your world, nothin but its very surface. . . . We've had lives like hard stones, dry on an uneasy way, we've had blinding flashes of dream and fear. And we ain't understood nothin but the very little things, we ain't said one word. . . . Life is obscene and empty, life is nothing, it can be any crazy fuckin thing. . . . Lord, why is man so free, so terribly free?

Man's whole life is a runaway. Everything. There is no definite word. No definite truth. No message to leave. Man is all. Man is endless. We are ready to die any minute of our lives, for it can't make no difference whether we know we're goina die or not. It's like a story of which the last part would be told too fast, and the teller says: and you see, after that, he dies. Period. No details. Not get down deep in that slow useless process of man being violently blown out. Too much bullshit.

He got to the cabin. It is about ten o'clock. Lester gets out and he hears Pearl's crazy voice yelling:

"Yeah, that's him, that's him."

He looks at the weird scene, thinking: I'm involved, all that crap is for me, but feeling terribly detached, as though the whole part had already been played. Then he notices that Lester is holding a rifle, and something flips and keeps blinking in him. That cat is crazy, he thinks. The whole family is mad! He looks at Lester's furious light-skinned face, and urgency is still beating in his head.

**212**

"Git the fuck outta here!" Lester shouted.

All that's phony, he thinks. . . .

"Dig, brer, I gotta stay here, I . . ."

There were about thirty feet between them. Something in Lester's attitude stiffened. He howled.

"DON'T YOU PLAY WITH THAT RIFLE, YOU CRAZY MOTHERFUCKER!

"Git goin, I said!"

That fool is goina shoot me, he thinks. For his crazy bitch of a wife. . . . He thinks of the mob behind him.

"AIN'T NO USE A'SHOOTIN', MAN!" He wants to get closer to them. He starts walking toward the cabin, very slowly. He keeps talking, loud, meanwhile.

"Ain't no use a'shootin', man, they after me anyhow. . . ." He realizes Lester can't hear him, maybe because of the wind, for he can see nothing in his attitude change while he's talking. Fright jumps down on him all of a sudden. He starts howling again.

"No! . . . No! . . . DON'T BE A FOOL, MAN! DON'T SHOOT!" And suddenly he thinks: if he kills me and they get here, they'll lynch HIM! He yells:

"No!"

And he starts running toward the cabin. There was a faint detonation in his chest as he saw Lester level the rifle. He fell down, feeling a hot and wet and burning and sticky and fast relaxation widen in his belly. And he suddenly had the whole wide sky above his eyes, he vaguely thought it was beautiful, but the sky was becoming wet and red too, and he thought: Lester, crazy sonofabitch. . . . But very slowly. And he tried to think again. He whispered: Ahma sleep now. Take that good old nap. His eyes winked, and he knew he was dying.